INVASION

WALTER DEAN MYERS

INVASION

 SCHOLASTIC PRESS

NEW YORK

Library of Congress Cataloging-in-Publication Data Available

ISBN 978-0-545-38428-5

10 9 8 7 6 5 4 3 2 1   13 14 15 16 17

Printed in the U.S.A.   23
First edition, October 2013

The text was set in Centaur.
Book design by Elizabeth B. Parisi and Kristina Iulo

For Christopher and Michael, may they always know peace

May 14, 1944

"Okay, so here's the deal, and listen carefully!"
Sergeant Duncan pushed the front of his helmet up and looked at his clipboard. "What we're going to do today is go to the ship, go down the rope ladders into the boat, and then go up the ladder back onto the ship. The brass wants to know how long it's going to take you to get back on the ship in case there's a last-minute change of plans."

"We're going to be marching all the way to the pier?" Gomez was short, but he looked like the hero in a Western movie.

"What, you got something better to do, pretty boy?"

"No, just wondering, Sarge."

"For some reason they're going to send some trucks to pick us up and take us to the boats," Duncan went on. "We're going to run through the exercise, and then they'll bring us back. General Gerhardt doesn't want Gomez to exhaust himself!"

"When are they going to stop reading our mail?" Kroll asked. "My girl feels like the Army is made up of Peeping Toms."

"Kroll, the only letters you get are from your mother, and she just writes because she's bored waiting for this thing to kick off."

"The whole battalion is going to get on the boats, then climb back on the ship?" I asked.

"I don't know, Woody, but when the colonel comes by, I'll tell him you have a question for him, okay?" Sergeant Duncan gave me the look and spit on the ground. "And wash your face before we start off; you don't want to scare any of the Navy guys. Any more questions?"

There was a lot of grumbling, but no questions.

"This is one of those stupid exercises they pull just so it looks good on paper," Sergeant Duncan said. "It's a wonder they don't have a bunch of Krauts standing around with stopwatches."

"If it's a maneuver to save our butts one day, you'll be glad to have the practice under our belt." MacIntyre was thirty, one of the oldest men in our outfit.

"Mac, are you practicing to be somebody's grandmother?" Sergeant Duncan asked. "Because that's *just* how you sound."

Duncan told us to relax until the trucks came. I had just settled on my cot with a bag of peanuts and a soda when the whistle blew to get up. I slung my backpack over one shoulder and went out with the others.

"Here they come," Gomez said, pointing down the road. "There's only about eight trucks, so it can't be the whole battalion going."

The trucks stopped about a hundred yards from where we were.

"What are they waiting for?" Gomez again.

"Probably waiting for some officer to get his fingers out of his rear end and tell them to start," Duncan said.

"They're moving again!" Minkowitz was blade thin and looked out of place in a uniform.

The trucks were standard two-and-a-half-ton jobs, or deuce and a halfs, as Duncan called them. They came in a close file, and then all made a simultaneous left turn so that they were facing away from us.

"They call that soldiering in Transportation," Sergeant Duncan said. "I call it bullshit."

"It's a black outfit," Stagg said. "Probably from Fort Meade."

"Nah, they keep all the Negroes down at Gordon in Georgia," Duncan said.

A driver and a passenger got out of each truck and stood at parade rest next to his vehicle. It was pretty sharp but, like the sergeant said, it wasn't much that anyone else couldn't have done. I thought I recognized one of the drivers. I looked closer as the Colored crews were given the command and opened the back tarpaulin flaps.

The one I thought I knew glanced over to where we stood. I did know him.

"Marcus!" I started toward him and saw him frown at first, then watched the frown turn into a big smile.

"Josiah Wedgewood! What the hell are you doing over here?" Marcus Perry put out his hand, and I grabbed it. "They gotta be desperate if they're going to let you do any of the fighting."

"They called me special to come over here and clean the Nazis out," I said. "You hear anything from home?"

"My mom said that they're rationing food up in Richmond," Marcus said. "How about you?"

"Man, Bedford, Virginia, seems like a whole lifetime ago," I said. "How long you been in England?"

"Two months of sitting around doing nothing," Marcus said.

"You still infantry?" I asked.

"No, I never was," Marcus said. "They sent me up to Fort Dix, and then down to Meade. I've been cleaning trucks night and day. I don't know if they expect us to drive them or sell them to the Germans. How about you?"

"Still infantry, still 29th. I got over here eight months ago and I'm ready for some action," I said. "I'd like to tell my folks what England looks like, but they won't let us put anything in our letters about where we are."

"Same here." Marcus leaned against the side of his truck. "Hey, wait, I did hear something from home. You know the Martin kid?

The one with the gap in his mouth? He took his car to Bud Speck's garage, and while he was showing him how it kept stalling, it started up and he ran over the mechanic's foot."

"You think there's something wrong with that boy?"

"Could be," Marcus said. "Oh, here's my boy, Grant. He's from Philadelphia."

Grant was a big dude, heavier and blacker than Marcus. He came over, and I shook his hand.

"You guys hear anything about when the invasion is going to kick off?" I asked.

Before Marcus could answer, Sergeant Duncan was up in my face. "Soldier, are you with the 29th Infantry?" he asked. "Because if you are, get your narrow little ass over there and get into one of those trucks!"

"Ride up in the cab with us," Marcus said. "You're skinny enough to fit."

I got in the cab with Marcus and started telling him what my mother had said, that the whole town was praying for us and hoping we would do well.

"We'll do all right," Marcus said. "How you like England?"

"To tell you the truth, I can't understand them half the time," I said.

"A guy started talking to me in a pub the other day, and I didn't understand a word he was saying," Marcus said. "He kept buying me beers and running his mouth, and I didn't know what he was talking about."

"I can't understand them none of the time," Marcus's friend Grant said. He was sitting between us. "I thought they were supposed to be talking all proper and shit."

"I can understand them in the movies," I said.

"There's five hours' difference between here and home," Marcus said as he started up the truck. "You know what I catch myself doing all the time? Figuring out what the folks back home are doing. Like it's nine o'clock here, but back home it's four in the morning. Everybody is still in bed."

"You thinking on what you're going to do when this is over?"

"I don't know, maybe go to college, or at least think about it." Marcus's truck was third in the line, and I noticed he kept a tight distance with the truck in front of him. "How about you?"

"I don't know, but I think I should be making some kind of decision," I said. "I was pretty good in art, but my dad doesn't think I can make any money off of it."

"Drawing pictures?" Marcus looked over at me.

"Yeah."

"Somebody got to draw them," he said. "Might as well be you."

"Hey, how come you guys got to go to a pub?" I asked. "They won't let us off the base."

"That's because they're only letting the Transportation Corps off the base," Marcus said, grinning. "We got a better image than you grunts."

"I think it's because they need us to win this war for them," I said. "We're not going to beat the Germans driving around."

"I might run over a few of them," Marcus said.

We reached the waterfront, and I hopped out of the truck. I felt great seeing Marcus and was still smiling as I lined up with the other guys from the 29th.

"How many times have we been up this damned gangplank?" Lyman was bitching again. "I could do this in my sleep."

There were some officers already on deck. I recognized Colonel Cawthon and Captain Arness. They told us to relax.

"Take five!" Cawthon called out. "Smoke them if you got them!"

Some of the guys started lighting up. There weren't any seats on the boats, so the men sat down right where they were. We had just about all got off our feet when somebody blew a whistle.

"One platoon, Baker Company, into the LCVP. Move it!"

There was the usual cussing as the thirty men from one platoon went to the side of the ship, over the low railing, and down the rope ladder into the small boat that was going to take us from the transport ships to the beach once the invasion actually started. I slung my rifle over my shoulder and looked at the men in the boat straightening themselves out. The guys with the semiautomatic weapons were up front, then the machine gunners, and then the rest of the guys with M1s and the soldiers carrying the mortars. There was just enough room for the men to stand facing forward without touching one another.

The LCVP pulled away about twenty feet, then the whistle blew again, and the sailor in the open wheelhouse brought the small craft back against the ship.

"Back on deck! Back on deck! Move it! Move it!" Captain Arness had a bullhorn this time.

Climbing up and down the ropes was pretty easy when the water was calm. You just had to watch out so that nobody stepped on your hand. I watched the men scramble back up the ropes quickly. A sergeant stopped at the top of the ladder and helped the others.

"You see that! You see that!" Cawthon was yelling. "That was perfect. Wrap it up, wrap it up."

The whole thing was over after the first try. Then somebody got the great idea that we should march back to our tents. I found Marcus before lining up with my platoon.

He took my hand and put his arm around my shoulders.

"When you write home, tell your mama you saw me," he said. "I'll do the same thing for you."

"Will do," I said.

"And take care of yourself," he added. There was some real seriousness in his voice.

"You know I'm going to do that," I said. "Those Germans haven't seen what Bedford men are about!"

Marcus and I shook hands again, and I told his friend it was nice meeting him, even though he hadn't said anything much.

The trucks took off without us, and we started double-timing back to our camp with Sergeant Duncan cursing every step of the way.

I'd known Marcus Perry most of my life. His high school football team was pretty good, maybe even as good as Moneta's, the school I had attended. Once when we were both working at Johnson's Hardware, we had talked about who would have won if the schools ever played each other. They didn't, of course, because he went to a Colored school, but it had been fun to talk about.

The trip back was brutal. The only time we rested was for five minutes, and then it was back on our feet again. We had to be carrying thirty pounds of gear. The M1 rifle weighed nine pounds all by itself.

I was in the best shape of my life. I was still skinny, but it was a hard skinny, and I felt good about it. I figured in a few months I'd start to grow a beard. At first I wouldn't trim it too much. Just let it grow out. Sometimes I would look into the mirror and think of myself as a soldier. I looked pretty good, or at least like somebody you wouldn't mess with.

The last mile or so was really hard. Some corporal I didn't know was pushing us, and guys were yelling at him to stop being so gung ho.

When we got in sight of the camp, the corporal spotted a platoon of engineers and increased the pace of the cadence until we were almost side by side with them.

"Yo, BA Company! We got a bunch of Girl Scouts to our left," our corporal shouted. "Can we beat them back to camp?"

We had already run almost a mile and nobody wanted to race, but nobody wanted the engineers to think they could beat us.

"Cadence count!"

Somebody started counting faster than we should have been running, but we all started moving faster. Then the sergeant jogging along with the engineers started picking up their pace, and in about the time it takes to spit on the ground we were racing that engineering company through the streets of southern England. Women that we passed turned and watched us and probably thought we were a bunch of fools — the weather was hot and humid, and here we were racing down the street as if it mattered.

We got back to the camp — which was really just a huge bunch of tents with barbed wire around them — a few seconds ahead of the engineers. Kroll, a decent kid from Jersey City, beat their lead man by fifteen feet. There was a lot of shouting and fist pumping. I let out a few yells, too, and then I threw up.

■ ■ ■

"Hey, Woody, you think the Germans are over there doing push-ups and crap while they're waiting for us to invade them?" Sergeant Duncan again. "I mean, what do you think they're thinking?"

"How can you tell what a German is thinking?" I asked. I had washed and brushed my teeth and was feeling almost human again. We had eggs and sausages for lunch, along with the usual Jell-O and ice cream, and I was feeling pretty good. "When I try to think about what they're thinking about, I have to imagine them thinking in German."

"People don't think in different languages," Duncan announced, as if he knew this for sure. "You think in pictures, not words."

I didn't know about that. I thought in words and I could think in pictures sometimes, and figured that the Germans must have done more or less the same.

My mind wandered to Marcus and how glad I was to see him, and then I started thinking about home. A stream of images came to mind. The corner of Bridge and Main where I got hit in the face by a sloshy snowball on my first day of high school. Green's Drug Store when me, Mom, and my younger brother, Ezra, went to get medicine for my father, and Mom didn't have enough money for the pills my father needed. The pharmacist said that he had some cheaper pills.

"They'll do the same thing," he said.

I was standing down a way from where Mom and Ezra were and I saw the pharmacist go behind the counter, wave the pills in the air, and bring them back to Mom. They were the same pills, he had just let Mom have them cheaper. That's the way things were in Bedford when I was little. It hadn't changed much, either, but I had.

After lunch I decided to write a letter to Mom and another one to Vernelle Ring. I wished I could have told them more about being in England, or what the English people were like. I thought they would have liked to know that the English drink their beer warm, drive on the wrong side of the street, and talk so damned fast you can't make out what they're saying half the time. But the censors just kept crossing stuff out, or even cutting it out.

It had taken most of my courage to write the first letter to Vernelle, and I knew I hadn't done a good job of letting her know how I felt about her. Well, maybe the truth was that I wasn't too sure how I felt about her. I liked her, and she was a nice kind of girl, but I didn't know if I loved her or anything like that.

"Hey, Woody, are you writing another letter?" Freihofer sat on the edge of his bunk, a towel over his head.

"Yeah, I'm writing to my mom," I said.

"So, what're you saying?"

"Why?"

"So I can write a letter to my mom," Freihofer said.

"I'm writing her that thirteen thousand American planes bombed Europe last week," I said.

"You can't write that," Freihofer said. "It'll be censored. That's like giving secret information to the enemy. What are you, a spy or something?"

"That's what it says in the *New York Times*," I said. "How secret can it be if it's in the *New York Times*?"

"You ever think that maybe the *New York Times* is a spy newspaper?"

"I'm also saying that Eisenhower thinks it's going to be an easy trip all the way through Germany," I said.

"The newspaper said that?" Freihofer asked.

"Yeah, he's telling the French people to stay off the roads to let us pass," I said.

"Yo! Duncan! You hear what Woody's saying? He said that Eisenhower is telling the Frenchies to stay off the roads when we get there!" Freihofer said. "If he says that even before the invasion begins, he's got to expect this whole thing to be short and sweet!"

"I told you that. Didn't I friggin' tell you that? This is a mop-up operation! The Germans don't want to fight." Duncan was nodding his big head up and down and scratching his crotch as he talked. "We walk in, we kick their tails all the way back to Sauerkrauten, then we mess with their women. Did you know that German women are all about six feet tall and blond?"

"That's good," Freihofer said. "I mean the easy part. I don't want to get into any heavy fighting."

"How can a country win a war when all their men walk like geese and they follow a little misfit who can't grow a mustache?" Duncan asked. "Did you know that the greatest German ever — that Beethoven guy — was deaf? He composed all their best songs and he was deaf! That make sense to you? Does that make sense to you, Woody?"

"No," I said.

"They beat the French in no time," Freihofer said. "But if Eisenhower is telling people to stay off the roads already, he must be pretty confident. Tell that to your mom, Woody. She'll be glad to hear it."

"She'll be even gladder to see me when I get back to Virginia," I said. "Me and Marcus, the black guy I was talking to today, signed up together, and then we went to my house and told my mom. She was crying, and laughing, and hugging us both. I was eighteen then, I'm nineteen now, and I'll probably be twenty before she sees me again."

"Your mom's a religious nut, right?" Duncan asked.

"No."

"Then how did you get a name like friggin' Josiah?"

"The family name is Wedgewood," I said. "Somebody in the family found out that we were vaguely connected to the British Josiah Wedgwood family that made dishes, and I got stuck with the name."

"What kind of dishes?"

"I don't know, plates and cups and saucers — stuff like that," I said, seeing that the conversation wasn't going too well.

"You're a nineteen-year-old, but you're skinny and young enough looking to be sixteen," Sergeant Duncan said. "And you're named after a friggin' cup! The Army is supposed to make men out of you boys, but you're never gonna make it, kid. You're never gonna make it."

I thought I was going to make it. What they said about the Germans not really wanting to fight, I believed that, too. I just couldn't see a Kraut standing up to an American.

Dolls in First!

"Okay, listen up!" Captain Bobby Joe Arness was a big man who looked like he might have played football somewhere. "There was a meeting this morning in which the whole invasion plan was laid out. To me, it sounds good. This is how this thing is going to work: The key is to deliver the maximum punch in the shortest amount of time. Move in, hit them hard, and keep hitting them! Don't let them regroup or even take a breather. What we've been waiting for is two days in a row of good weather so we can make sure that everybody gets into place when and where they're supposed to be. This is going to be a team effort, and we're going to be the first on the field."

"Why do we need two days?" Sergeant Duncan asked. "If the first day goes good, the rest of the guys can come in on tugboats if they got to."

"Duncan, I think Eisenhower knows a little more about this than we do. He's sending in the 101st, our paratroopers, in waves," Arness said. "A lot of their men are going in the night before the invasion with specific objects in mind. They'll also be sending in dolls all along the coastline as a distraction."

"Did you say *dolls?*" a soldier still lying in one of the top bunks asked.

"What would you do if you saw a doll come floating down from the sky, soldier?" Arness asked.

"Shoot the shit out of it!" was the quick answer. "And wonder what the Americans were sending out dolls for!"

"Exactly," Arness answered. "You'd be wasting ammunition shooting at dolls and you'd be thinking instead of fighting against the guys coming at you from a different direction. Got it?"

"If you say so."

"Then the rest of the 101st will go in with us and a ranger battalion. We need two days of good weather so we don't send the airborne in and then cancel our landing because of bad weather.

"So the airborne goes in the night before, then the bombers hit them, and then we go in and finish the job. Any questions?"

"Yeah. It took you three minutes to tell us," a corporal said. "How come your meeting with the brass took three hours?"

A couple of the guys laughed, and Captain Arness even grinned.

"They made us review, and memorize, some of the beach maps," Arness said. "Each assault unit has their own plans and routes to get off the beach and into the surrounding areas. Sergeant Major Ravell of the Royal Scots Fusiliers will tell you what to expect on approaching the beach."

The Scottish soldier stood up and looked at us. He wasn't more than five feet five, but he was stocky. He didn't move his head once he stood up, but his eyes darted around the room. For a long time he didn't say anything, either, just looked at us. After a while it got to be a little silly, and some of our guys started smiling.

"I'm going to try to talk with an American accent," he said. His voice was high and thin. "I'll talk the best I can, and you listen the best you can. When you hit the beaches we don't want any surprises. Anything that holds you up from getting on the beach and getting your weapons in action could cause you to go down.

"The first obstacle you have to deal with is the water. Depending on where the boat stops, you might be in as much as three to four feet of water when the ramp drops. Hopefully, you'll be in closer. Then there are obstacles in the water: poles pointing toward the shore so the boats will run up on them and either tip over or hang up on them. Some are just logs driven into the seabed; others are more elaborate iron structures that look like . . ." He turned to Captain Arness. "What did your major call them?"

"Jacks," Captain Arness said. "They have little spikes sticking out at different angles. Only these are seven to eight feet high. Then there are rolls of barbed wire just to make life difficult for you. Hopefully, a lot of this will have been cleared away by the bombers. The bombing should leave craters for you in case there is any return fire."

"Some of the obstacles have mines attached to them," Ravell said. "They're called Teller mines, but the bombing before you land should clear a lot of that away. The bombs will set off any mines they've got buried on the beaches, too. The Germans had a few floating mines in the water, but they've been there a long while, and I know that some of them aren't any good anymore. Once you get past the barbed wire, you're on French soil."

"How do you know all this?" Sergeant Duncan asked. "The Krauts send you a full report?"

"No, Yank, I've been on reconnaissance missions on these beaches four times in the last two months," Ravell said. "I've come up in four different places, swimming underwater. I've looked at the mines, disarmed the ones that I could handle safely, and made drawings of their defenses. Plus, we have a great deal of information from the French Resistance. But nobody was shooting at me when I was over there swimming around, so it's liable to be a lot different when the actual landings start."

"Thanks, Sergeant Major." Captain Arness stood and shook the Scottish soldier's hand.

"And thank you, Captain," Ravell said. "And *sláinte* to all of you."

Ravell left, and Captain Arness continued.

"We all know which assault team we're on. We should just about know where the Vierville Draw, the road leading into the town, lies.

We might or might not get some resistance, but the road should be pretty obvious. There's a steep area on either side of the draw, so they've probably got it zeroed in, and there might be some heavy fighting until we kill off their artillery. But we will get through, and once we do we set up defensive perimeters in and around Vierville and put down any forces still trying to shell the beach. Anybody got questions?"

"Yeah, sir. Did that Tommy actually go up on the beach like he said?" Petrocelli from Bayonne, New Jersey, was wide-eyed, as if he didn't believe Ravell.

"He's actually walked up on the beach and met with some of the French Resistance fighters," Arness said. "He knows what he's talking about. But don't let it sound too easy. The tricky thing will be to find the draws after we land. We can see where they are on the maps, but all of the landmarks should be obliterated by the time we land."

"By the bombers?" Lyman asked.

"By the bombers," Arness said. "If everything goes well there might not be any landmarks, and we'll just have to sort ourselves out once we're on the beach. It shouldn't be a big deal. You know your officers and you know what the problems are. We have to get on the beach and off of it so that the next wave of men can land as well as the supplies."

"And the Germans don't have any idea of what's going on?" Sergeant Duncan asked.

"They've got a damned good idea of what's going on, Duncan. They know we're coming, but they don't know when and they have a thousand miles of coastline to cover. Every day we're getting intelligence about where they think we're going to land."

"How do we know we're not just a decoy?" Minkowitz asked. "And maybe the real attack will be somewhere else?"

"Could be, soldier, but wherever *you* land, you give them hell, okay?"

"Yes, sir."

"The big brass thinks that we should be well established around Vierville within six hours," Arness went on. "Or at least that's when they start sending in the dancing girls to entertain us."

"If it's going to be this easy, why don't the Krauts just give up?" Stagg asked.

Stagg was a hardcase, as my grandfather back in Bedford would have called him. He didn't speak to anybody unless he had to, and nobody spoke to him because we didn't want to.

"Eisenhower is giving them that option," Arness said. He looked satisfied. "We're dropping thousands of leaflets telling them that it might be a good idea to pack it in while they're still breathing."

I was feeling good about the invasion. I had read about how the Nazis had moved across Europe, crushing people and carting some of them off to work camps. But, like Sergeant Duncan had said, they had never gone up against anybody like the United States Army. I knew our guys in the 29th were ready. Mostly country boys, we weren't ones to shy away from a good fight when we had God and the country on our side.

The papers were talking about how our planes were blowing up their oil fields in Italy. Over two thousand planes had moved in from Africa and bombed the Germans and what was left of the Italian army silly.

By the time Captain Arness left, we were all feeling a little puffy around the gills and pleased with ourselves. All except Stagg, who looked at everything suspiciously.

I wrote to Vernelle again. I was so full of myself that it was all I could do not to propose marriage to her right then and there. I knew I couldn't tell her exactly where I was or anything, or how the invasion was going to go, but I did tell her that maybe I could get to see her on my birthday. She had to know that it was in October, so if she put two and two together she could have figured out when I'd be leaving to head back home.

I also thought about writing to a few other girls, but then I thought better of it. No use in writing to a girl if you don't know how she's going to take it. I didn't want to go home and find a half-dozen women thinking they were going to marry me!

■　■　■

We were halfway through supper — which consisted of roast beef, peas, carrots, chicken stew, some lettuce with pink stuff on it, and ice cream — when my stomach started growling. I cleaned my tray off and headed right to the latrine.

If there's anything I can't get used to it's sitting on a GI John. In our john they had a long trough to piss in along one wall and ten toilets along the other wall. The toilets were really just benches, about a foot and a half high, with holes for your butt. Each hole was over another, deeper, hole in the ground. They filled the holes in the ground with lime and dirt to keep the stink down, but that didn't keep the flies from eating you up alive if you had to sit there for any length of time. Anyway, I didn't like doing my business in front of six or seven other guys. I guess I'm just funny that way.

But going right after dinner wasn't too bad because it was only me and Mac, and he never said anything to anybody anyway. Mac was in the john, reading a paperback book and smoking his pipe. It was like he was at home or something.

"What're you reading?" I asked.

"*For Whom the Bell Tolls*," he said. "Hemingway."

"Shouldn't that be *For* Who *the Bell Tolls*?" I asked.

Mac gave me a look and shook his head. I didn't like that.

Some whistles blew and I heard some guys running around outside the latrine. I figured it was another alert — we had one every two days or so — or another stupid night drill. It wasn't; it was another march off to the ships.

"Okay, guys, drop your cocks and grab your socks!" Sergeant Duncan was yelling outside the latrine. "We're going again!"

This would be the fourth time we had started off for the invasion, sometimes not even getting to the ships before it was called off.

"What day is this?" Mac asked me.

"I think it's Saturday," I said.

"No, it's later than that," Mac said. "I had a *Stars and Stripes* for Saturday already."

"Could be," I said. "I still think they're going to wait until the Fourth of July before they actually have the real invasion."

"If I were a German, that's what I'd think," Mac answered, pulling his pants up. "And I'd probably be right."

We had to keep our packs ready and stowed, so all I had to do was check it and buckle it up. We had each been issued twenty clips of ammo — with 8 rounds in a clip, that's 160 rounds apiece. A couple of guys had carbines with 15 rounds, but I didn't like them. The M1 rifle had more kick, and it would shoot no matter what you did with it.

We lined up and kind of half marched, half walked from the camp area for the two and a half miles to the transport ships. The night was clear and a little cool. As we had our names checked off going up the ramp onto the ship, I got a funny feeling. I told Lyman that I thought we were really going this time.

"Why do you think that?" he asked.

"Just a feeling," I said. Lyman looked a little flaky to me, a little too good-looking, maybe, and I always wondered what he was thinking.

"You scared?" he asked.

"Of what?"

"Of getting shot or something," he said.

"No, not really," I said. "I just want to get it over. You know what we should do?"

"What?"

"Let's ask Duncan for a leave now," I said. "We'll put our bid in now, and soon as the fighting's over maybe we can take some time off in Paris."

"He'll give you a leave because he wants you to draw him messing with some girls," Lyman said. "Me, I'm not sure."

"Okay, here's the deal. I got it figured out to a tee." Duncan again. "We land on the beach, and then everybody jumps up and down, see? With all of the equipment we're carrying, the whole country will flip over. Then the Germans *and* the French will go flying over the channel and into England. Then the Brits will beat the crap out of the Krauts while we sit up in Normandy and have parties."

"We've got so much gear because we have to clear the beach right away," Captain Arness said. "All the first assault teams are supposed to be off the beach within three hours."

"Captain, no disrespect, sir." Victor Polucci was a pimply-faced guy from Pennsylvania. "But I like Sergeant Duncan's plan better. We jump up and down, flip the country, and toss all the Germans over the channel. Then, if they want to get back to France, it's their problem, not ours."

"Well, you work on that plan, soldier," Captain Arness said. "When you get the details ironed out, give it to me and I'll pass it upstairs."

The Navy has a boat for everything, even small boats to take you out to their big boats. We started off toward the *Thomas Jefferson*, the transport ship that was supposed to take us across the channel to Normandy, in good spirits. We had started this trip before, only to have the whole thing called off. On shore there were soldiers loading trucks, stacking crates of ammunition, and others waiting for the landing craft and utility boats to take them to whatever transport would take them to Europe.

In my heart I thought there were good signs that things were going to work out for us. We were boarding the *Thomas Jefferson* on Sunday, a good day to start anything. And Jefferson, besides being the third president of the United States, was a Virginia man who had lived only eighty miles from Bedford. He had understood what liberty was about, and he would have understood what we were doing better than just about anyone.

"When we left from New York to come to England, they had a band playing for us and a bunch of pretty girls waving their handkerchiefs," Minkowitz said.

"Maybe the Germans will have a band waiting for us in France," Duncan said.

I didn't think that was so funny, but I didn't want to get into it with Duncan. He was a wiseass, but I liked him.

We had to climb up the rope ladders to get on the *Thomas Jefferson*. The sailors waiting for us had lists of where we would bunk, and we made our way down into the cabin area. The gray iron stairs were hard to maneuver down with our backpacks and rifles, and the sleeping area was dingy and dark, but we got to stow our gear and stretch out for a while. The bunks were four deep, and Minkowitz said he was glad he wasn't on the bottom bunk.

"If the guy on the top bunk gets seasick and throws up, it's got to go somewhere," he said.

I knew how important our mission was, and how dangerous it was going to be. No matter what happened, some of us might not make it back. The officers were called for another meeting, and the rest of us just sat around. Some of the guys shook hands and wished one another luck. Mostly we were pretty calm. One guy — I knew him from the National Guard — got upset when he found he didn't have his spare socks with him.

"What the fuck did I do with them?" He was searching through his backpack.

"You're from around Bedford, aren't you?" I asked, throwing him a pair of my socks.

He looked up at me, tried to figure out what I was saying, then took a deep breath and kind of calmed down. "Yeah, Moneta," he said. "You from Bedford?"

"Yep, best little town in the world," I said, extending my hand.

"Kemprowski," he said, shaking my hand. "Carl Kemprowski. My sister was runner-up in the Miss Virginia pageant a few years ago."

"Wedgewood. My friends call me Woody."

"You got one of those names you have to have a nickname to cover up," he said. He looked at the pair of rolled socks I had thrown him. "Thanks, but I think I'll find mine," he said, tossing them back. "I was just kind of distracted packing all of this other gear. Man, they've got us carrying everything except the kitchen sink."

I told him if he didn't find his I'd share mine, and he thanked me again.

Afterward, Sergeant Burns pulled me aside and told me not to give anybody my socks.

"You got to learn to take care of yourself," he said. "If that guy's careless, you need to let it be on him."

For some reason Burns seemed pissed, and I didn't answer him.

We had Navy chow — potatoes, peas, slices of beef, Jell-O, and ice cream. Not bad. We would have done better on shore eating Army chow, but it wasn't bad.

After supper, a chaplain — his name tag read SANTORA — came to our bunk area and said that he was going to hold a prayer service on deck in fifteen minutes.

"It'll be nondenominational," he said. "So anybody who's a believer can come."

I had gone to services in the morning at the Protestant chapel, but I went up on deck and found where Captain Santora was holding his service. There wasn't much to it, just Santora asking God to protect us all.

When I got back to my bunk, I saw Burns and Minkowitz still in the area. Minkowitz was reading, as usual, and Burns was sharpening his bayonet.

"You actually think you're going to stick somebody with that thing?" I asked.

"If I run out of bullets, I'll stick them with the bayonet," Burns said. "If I lose the bayonet, I'll fight them with my fists. If they cut my hands off, I'll bite the fuckers!"

"How was the prayer service?" Minkowitz asked.

"Good," I said.

"Mark Twain once wrote an essay about war prayers," Minkowitz said. "He said when you pray to God to save your life, you're praying for him to kill your enemy. And your enemy is praying for God to kill you."

"That's depressing," I said.

"Yeah, I guess," Minkowitz said.

"Hey, what do your friends call you?"

"Mink," he answered. He looked embarrassed.

I lay on my bunk and wondered what the guys around me were thinking. Some were reading, others were talking quietly, some were writing letters. That's the way the ship was, subdued. No one was making too much noise until six o'clock. Then a sergeant came in and announced the invasion was being postponed.

"Bad weather," he said. "Ike just sent a note to the Germans not to wait up for us."

"I bet we sit here for two days," Minkowitz said. "And then we get off and go back to the staging area."

"One of the Army photographers said that he thought we weren't going to have the invasion until Bastille Day, the fourteenth of July," the sergeant who had told us of the postponement said. "That's French Independence Day. That way it'll look good in the history books."

That made a little sense, and I liked being part of an invasion to free Europe that began on a historic day. It was patriotic. I imagined my folks sitting around in the backyard, maybe having sandwiches or something, and hearing the news.

■ ■ ■

I slept good, even though I woke up a few times. When you wake up in a ship, all you can see is the red light near the bottom of the stairs leading up to the compartments above. I could hear the water against the sides of the ship, and sometimes the ship seemed to groan, as if it was struggling to get somewhere.

It was dark and cold when we got up in the morning, and I had the worst breakfast I had ever had. It was watery scrambled eggs, two dried-up little sausages, something that looked like grits with corn in it, toast, and coffee so thick the milk didn't even make it lighter.

An officer tried to get us to do calisthenics on deck, but everybody went about it halfheartedly. If we weren't already in shape, we certainly wouldn't get in shape doing toe touches on the transport.

Most of the morning we just sat around. Some of the Navy guys had girly magazines, and we passed them around. Then they set up a screen and started showing newsreels of baseball games, and we watched them until after lunch (also terrible). A tech corporal named Davis tried to start a pool on when we would start off. He was explaining it when one of the Navy guys pointed out to sea.

"They're taking down the nets!" he yelled.

"What does that mean?" I asked him.

"They're taking down the nets they put out to stop submarines from entering the harbor," he said. "That means we're moving out."

The rail was soon lined with guys from the 29th looking out toward the English Channel. Some of the transports were already moving, and in the distance I could see two sleek destroyers, dark against the grayness of the day, slide across the horizon. We were on our way!

Long day. Everybody is edgy. Everybody is a little sick in the stomach.

I checked my watch. It was 4:17 P.M. on the fifth of June, 1944.

The mood on the ship, which had ranged from boredom to irritation, grew quiet again. You could almost feel the men going deep into themselves. A captain came around telling us not to forget to take our seasick pills in case the water was choppy.

"How soon do they work?" Petrocelli asked.

The captain shrugged, then said something about thirty minutes. We all knew he was guessing.

Some guys set up a crap game, rolling the dice on a blanket. Sergeant Duncan looked like he was winning some money.

I imagined going to Paris with Duncan. I knew he would probably look for girls. If I was definitely engaged to Vernelle, it would have been wrong to fool around with a French girl, but I wasn't really engaged to her yet. In fact, she hadn't answered my letters, so I didn't know what she thought of me.

Supper was stupid, with peas, chicken, and cold French fries. Minkowitz wondered if that was how the Navy always ate.

"I got a feeling that as soon as we head toward the beach, they're going to break out the good stuff," he said.

"When they put you out to sea for six months, you forget what the good stuff is," Sergeant Duncan said. "After a while, stale bread gets to tasting good."

Taking my boots off felt good, and so did stretching out on my bunk as I lay down. I saw Abbott and Davis get out of their clothes and look as if they had settled in for the night. Somebody was playing a portable radio, good swing music, and we listened to that for a while. Bedford came to mind again. It would be twelve thirty, and guys on the early shift at the laundry where I had worked summers would just be getting back from lunch. Maybe they would be thinking about us, wondering what we were doing and if we were okay.

I started thinking about my mom. Eleven thirty and she would be home, cleaning and maybe listening to *Our Gal Sunday* on the radio. She wouldn't be worried if she hadn't heard anything. None of her letters mentioned the invasion, and I didn't even know if she knew I was going to be a part of it. If she did, she might have just pushed it out of her mind, the way she did sometimes.

"There's no use in worrying yourself about milk that's already spilled or whether somebody else's pancakes are going to rise," she would say.

Even if she was worried sick about something, she wouldn't let on as if she was.

My brother, Ezra, would know about the invasion. He was smart, maybe smarter than me. I wanted to bring him something from France. A souvenir. Maybe I could pick up a few and give them to Ezzie, Dad, Uncle Joe, and maybe even something for Vernelle.

If the 29th did all right, if we made the newspapers, I thought Dad would be proud of me. He was happy that I had come home to join up. Some of the guys from his job had asked him, and he had told them he didn't know if I was man enough to fight for my country or not. On the night before I left for England, he had taken me out on the back porch and poured a drink for himself and one for me. He didn't say anything, just poured the two drinks, and we sat there drinking them for a while, and then he said, "Good night, son," and went to bed.

I didn't know what it was supposed to mean, really. I guessed it was supposed to be some kind of man thing. He and Uncle Joe had fought in the First World War, and he had said it had been his obligation as a man.

The Navy quarters, with guys stacked four high, was dark and stinky. We were too close together, and there wasn't any air two stories below the deck. I wasn't scared or anything, just anxious to get it on and over with.

They got us up at a little past two in the morning. I tried to sense if the ship was still moving, and it felt as if it was. No one was talking. We got dressed, then went up for breakfast. Actually, we went up about five steps and into another compartment, and down five steps to get to the mess hall. Franks, beans, scrambled eggs, and toast.

Two thirty we were told to shut up and listen to a message. It was from General Eisenhower. It was serious and short. He said he expected nothing less than victory, and something about God being on our side. At least that's what I think he said; I was getting a little too nervous to think a lot.

We were told to scrape our trays into the garbage and put them on the rack to be washed. Sergeant Duncan said the Navy could go have intercourse with itself and left his tray on the table. Most of the rest of us did, too.

I got my gear, and Lord, it seemed heavier than when we were climbing up onto the deck the day before. We went up the narrow passageways — we couldn't even go two at a time — and assembled in teams. Then Colonel Cawthon called out the boat numbers and we climbed into the landing craft.

On some ships they had the landing craft come alongside and you climbed down the rope ladders into the smaller boat. On the *Thomas*

Jefferson you loaded onto the boat on deck and then they hauled you over the side and lowered the boat into the water. It didn't make any difference to me.

The *Thomas Jefferson* was rocking from side to side from the choppiness of the water. It was cold, especially for June, and some of the men were already getting seasick.

"Where's Lady?" One of the men in the boat in front of us was looking for his dog. They found the dog and put her in the boat just before the crane started lifting it.

The boats were lifted over the side and lowered into the sea. When our boat went off the deck, we were all holding on. The sky was beginning to lighten, and I felt good for a moment. It was only for a moment, though, because just then the ships started sending a barrage of heavy artillery onto the shore. We were over the rail, and men turned to see what they could of the beach.

"How far is the beach?" Captain Arness asked.

"Ten miles!" came the quick answer from the Navy guy in the small wheelhouse. There were two sailors at the open wheelhouse, one on the wheel and another on what looked like a .50 caliber machine gun. A third sailor was in the front of the craft.

"Make sure your life preservers are free!" somebody yelled.

We all had on rubber tubes wrapped around our waists in case the boat capsized. I checked mine, and it was slipping down under my canteen. I tried to pull it up, but it was stuck. No problem; I could swim good.

The winch let our boat down and I thought that would be good, but the sea just started tossing it up and down.

There were two big Navy ships, the *Texas* and the *Arkansas*. Their guns were sending streaks of flames across the breaking dawn toward the beaches. My throat went dry, and I realized I was holding my breath. I opened my mouth to breathe easier.

There was no place to sit and not much to hold on to, so when the engine of the landing craft started, some of the men in front fell. The sailor driving the boat spun it around and away from the *Thomas Jefferson* and headed straight toward the beach, then turned and joined other boats that were going in a circle. We couldn't see anything straight ahead because the ramps were too high, but when the boats turned we could see over the sides pretty good. All I wanted to see was the beach we were supposed to land on.

Somebody behind me threw up, and nobody wanted to turn and look at him. It was too late now. We were in the water and committed. Somebody, I thought it was Petrocelli, started saying the Lord's Prayer.

Our Father, who art in heaven,
Hallowed be thy name.
Thy Kingdom come,
Thy will be done
On Earth, as it is in Heaven.
Give us this day our daily bread,

And forgive us our trespasses
As we forgive those who trespass against us,
And lead us not into temptation,
But deliver us from evil.

We were being tossed around on the water. The noises of the big naval guns rumbled across the overcast sky, and the roar of the LCVP's engines filled me with a kind of dread. It was like a huge drumroll announcing that I was about to do something momentous. There were waves banging against the front of the ramp and water coming in over the sides. As we moved away from the *Thomas Jefferson* the tossing calmed down a bit, but it was still a rough ride. My field jacket was getting drenched, and I was getting colder by the minute.

We headed to a clearing between the transports where there were three other boats beginning to form a circle. It was the same as it had been in practice, the boats circling until we were ready to make a charge for the beach. Then they would straighten out into a skirmish line and go hell-bent for leather until we hit land, or until the obstacles stopped us.

I wasn't really scared, just nervous. It had all gone well in practice, but I knew we hadn't had any opposition off the coast of England, or when we had first tested the landings down at Virginia Beach.

"When the ramp drops, get out quick, but go in low." Duncan's voice danced over the noise. "Don't bunch!"

I knew enough to keep my head down, and I knew better than to bunch up and make an easy target group for the Germans.

"First team's gone!"

A Company was on its way. I thought of the guys in that group, good men. They always thought of themselves as the best in the battalion, and I knew they would try to prove it today.

I checked the watch the Army had issued me. We had thirty minutes before we followed A Company. If everything went well, the boats that carried them in would be headed back out to the transports to pick up another team as we neared the beach.

"Where are the friggin' planes?" Lyman's voice was nasal and whiny enough to cut through the noise.

"Maybe they're already . . ."

I didn't know if I just lost the rest of the sentence in the growing din of sound and wind, or if whoever had started it had just stopped talking. Somehow it wasn't a time for talking.

I went over my job. Get on the beach, find some cover, and lay down covering fire while the mortars and machine guns were setting up. Then get to the road that led to Vierville-sur-Mer, get myself up the road and onto the perimeter of the city. Then we'd check our squads, clean up any Kraut resistance that A Company had missed, and cordon off a supply space so the next waves could bring more supplies onto the beach.

I caught myself breathing shallowly and tried to relax. The man next to me was hunching his shoulders, jerking them up really, and

I was glad to see that somebody was as nervous as I was. Kroll, ahead to my right, turned back. He smiled, and I nodded. He was doing something to the end of his M1, and I saw it was a condom he was putting over the end to keep the water out. I had already put my rifle barrel down to keep the water out, and reminded myself to turn it up as we got near the beach.

The Navy guy driving the boat was yelling into his radio. I was hoping he was on top of things and knew what to do. Then he signaled a fat Navy guy who was in the well with us. The fat guy, who was wearing a Mae West, climbed up to the wheelhouse and snatched the cover off the fifty.

I said a prayer. *Oh, Jesus, let me do okay. Please.*

The boats, which had been circling, now began to form lines facing the beach we were going to attack. I looked at my watch. I couldn't believe the thirty minutes between assault teams had passed so fast!

We were forming a skirmish line, and it looked as if we were the third boat from the left. Was that right? I couldn't remember if we were supposed to be the third or fourth. I did know that if we landed on target, the road would only be fifteen to twenty feet to my right. Two first downs and I would be all right. The LCVP started moving ahead, jerking the front end up as we started toward the section of Omaha Beach they had labeled Easy Red.

It was supposed to take an hour to reach the beach, which meant that A Company and the boats to our right had thirty minutes before touching land. I was breathing shallow again, but this time I just went with it. I had a job to do, and I didn't want to mess it up.

The water was rough and the boat was bouncing over and through the waves. Men were falling forward and trying to catch themselves, and I knew some would be damn near too seasick to fight. My stomach was queasy, but I was more nervous than sick.

Sixty minutes of trying to calm myself down, of trying to keep my breakfast down, of trying to remember what I was supposed to be doing once I hit the beach. Everybody was holding on to the sides of the boat. We'd have to form our team positions once the ramp dropped, and we didn't want to be lying on the deck when it was time to get out.

"The Germans are firing!" Davis had climbed up on the side of the boat. "There's shit coming out toward us!"

"Get your ass down from there, soldier!"

Davis got down and tightened his chin strap. I tightened mine, and then loosened it, and then tightened it again. I started checking my gear. I couldn't feel my hands too good because they were cold and wet. I opened them and closed them quickly a few times, as we used to do in Virginia in the wintertime. It didn't help much, but I knew it didn't matter. I could see, I could pull a trigger, I could run.

The math was easy: two hundred and fifty yards from the water to the draw, maybe another forty if we had to run at an angle. Even with combat boots and equipment it shouldn't take more than two minutes. The guys lugging the machine guns, which weighed about fourteen pounds, and the tripods, which weighed over forty, would be slower, but that's why I was supposed to lay down covering fire.

"If the enemy has to keep his head down to keep it from being blown off, he can't shoot you!" Stagg had said a thousand times. "Keep the Kraut's head down and you'll save your ass!"

I looked at my watch. A Company had hit the beach! I said another quick prayer to God and asked him to kill as many Germans as possible. The hell with Mark Twain!

Our division would do well, I was sure. They were 29th and proud. I was 29th and proud, too. We'd do Virginia proud.

"In your files! In your files!"

We closed our positions and crouched as we neared the beach. In the background I heard the Navy guns sound off again. They seemed closer than they had before. I wanted to turn and look to see if I could see the ships, but my body wouldn't move.

A series of *pings* hit the side of the boat, and I looked up and saw a row of bullet holes nearly two feet long. Jesus!

To our left, two LCVPs, one smoking badly, were headed back out to sea.

A loud *thump!* and our boat went up high, nearly turned over, and then came crashing down. Everyone was sprawled on the deck. Another series of shots hit the side of the boat, and I felt us lurching sideways. The back of our boat had swung around so that we were parallel to the beach instead of facing it!

The ramp dropped, rattled as it got caught up, and hit the water with a loud *bang!*

"Everybody out! Everybody out! Let's go, 29!"

Hit the Beach!

Out of the boat. Cold water rushing against my legs. Water going into my boots. I am stumbling forward. I am shaking.

"Let's go! Let's go!" someone is shouting.

Something brushes against my legs. I look down — an arm! The bloody socket still bleeding. Red specks, red specks of blood on the white foam.

Oh my God!

I look toward the beach. It seems miles ahead. To my right an amphibious vehicle burns. Smoke pours out from its side. The top opens and a soldier starts to climb out. His arms wave in the air. The churning sea buries his cries. I see his body jerk and go back as he is hit. Other arms push his lifeless body out. They are trying to climb out, away from the flames. The next soldier is hit in the head. The Germans have the vehicle zeroed in.

"Move out! Get to the beach!" someone is calling out.

Move. I tell myself to move. My legs are heavy as they fight against the water. I think that I am crying.

Oh my God! Oh my God!

I start toward the beach. Each step is like lifting a huge weight. My feet are unsteady as I push myself forward.

My heart is racing. I am gasping for air. Gasping! I hear the *pop! pop!* of bullets going past me. My eyes are narrowed, almost closed. I can't see as I wait for the bullet that will end my life. Push the feet forward.

"Move! Move!"

An ugly explosion, a spout of dark water and black smoke, lifts a DUKW from the water. It turns over like a huge turtle in agony and falls on its back. I know the crew is dead. They never had a chance. Never saw France. The blast makes me change direction. I am going sideways, confused.

"Come on, guys! We got 'em! We got 'em!" Sergeant Duncan waves us forward. Then . . . then . . . his shoulders rise in the water. Almost as if he is going to fly away. His body turns, and I can see he has been hit. His body is tossed backward, toward me. There is a huge hole in the top of his chest. Blood pumps in short spurts from the wound. I am almost in a state of panic, but I look at his face.

The mouth is open, twisted. He might be screaming. I can't hear him. For a moment I look into his eyes.

"Move! Move!" someone is shouting.

I turn away from Sergeant Duncan. Half filled with panic and half filled with shock. I am not mourning Duncan, I am mourning myself; I think I am dead.

The shore is less than a hundred yards away. I can see men running up the beach. Some fall at once, silently, sliding backward into the cold sea. Some throw their arms into the air to fall in a spasm of pain. Others fall quietly, as if they were tired.

I am so scared! I am so scared!

There are explosions on the beach to my right. Tanks burning. There are men crouched behind the tanks. I run, and the water is lower. Bullets trace a straight line next to me. Little spouts of water fly up, fly past. I am still alive. My eyes are stinging. I push my legs forward. I am pushing as hard as I can. What have we got into? A body is in the water ahead of me. He's lost his helmet. His wound is dark. There is a hole in his pale white face.

Oh my God!

His wound looks like a third eye. It is grotesque. I am so scared. I am so fucking scared. I turn away from him.

Fifty yards from the beach.

There is a steel beam, as tall as me, sticking up. Three men are crouched at its base. The bullets slam against the iron. Someone has seen the men trying to hide. Someone is trying to kill them.

"Keep moving! Keep moving!"

The water is less deep, and my knees begin to bend. I am trotting. I want to live. The water is below my knees and the ground is firmer. I see someone facedown in the shallow water. He is alive and struggling to get up. It's Minkowitz.

I grab him and try to pull him along with me.

"Leave him, he's dead!" I look up and see Stagg. He's pointing toward the beach. "Move! Move!" he barks at me.

Minkowitz's face is pleading as he tries to struggle up. I can't leave him. I pull at his shoulders. He grunts, and I think he's crying.

Suddenly someone is grabbing his other shoulder. It's Stagg. He pulls Minkowitz forward with a jerk, and I am pulling his other shoulder. Minkowitz comes to life, his legs move, and he stumbles to his feet. We are all running.

We are at the water's edge. A soldier runs past us onto the sand. Suddenly he falls to his knees and clutches his belly. As his body bends forward, I see the bullets rip into his bowed back. We move away from him. Move away from the terrible bullets.

We have reached the sand. There are bodies everywhere. Men are dead or dying, their legs and arms sometimes flung out, sometimes tucked under their lifeless bodies. Some are crying out.

Oh my God! Oh my God!

There is a group of men huddled against the base of the cliffs, and I run toward them. I think I can make it when suddenly something hits me. My rifle shatters with a clanging noise, and I fall forward. Quickly someone is pulling me up. Somehow my legs bend and I am running. My rifle bangs against my knees. I reach the base of the cliff and fall down among the other men.

I look at them. They look at me. We are dazed, confused, terrified. Looking back at the sea, I see more boats coming in. Some are hit before they lower the ramps. One boat comes in close. The ramp is lowered and we can see the men screaming. Their screams are silent in the distance as the storm of chaos drowns out their dying.

A shell hits the beach fifty yards away, sending up sand and debris. It is too far away to affect us, but we cringe. I feel myself moving against the boots of the soldier behind me.

There is a soldier walking along the beach; he stops and kneels next to a wounded man, does something to his wound, and quickly moves on. For a moment I think he is Jesus, but then I see he's a medic.

Two men are trying to set up a mortar. They get the pieces together and set off one round, and then another. They begin to argue, and somebody says they haven't armed the shells. It's like throwing a rock at the enemy.

Another shell hits. It's closer than the first, but still away.

"They're trying to zero in on us!" Stagg's voice is familiar. "They're walking the shells in."

I reach for my rifle and see that it's shattered. They've shot my rifle, and the stock is splintered. The barrel is twisted. That's how close I was to death. The rifle, across my chest, took the bullets that were meant to end my war.

I don't know if anybody can see my tears. I know they are there. Maybe they are falling inside.

I don't want to look at the small stretch of beach I have just crossed. But I do. I am trembling, and I am crying. There are bodies everywhere. Medics are running from man to man, trying to see if any are still alive. Sometimes an arm or leg moves, but there is no sure life in the figures.

There are still soldiers everywhere. Their lifeless bodies scare something inside of me. I am trembling. Some of the bodies look as if they are reaching for something. What could it be? I don't want to see them, but I can't look away. When I look away I still see them.

A medic is hit and falls to his knees. He is crawling away from the man he had hoped to save. More bullets hit the medic and he is still. We are in a killing zone, and we are dying. Beyond the edge of the beach, where the sand blurs with the water's edge, there are more bodies. The waves move them in and out, turn them, mock them. And farther still, there are more boats coming in.

One blows up as it is hit. . . . By what? A mortar shell? Fate? The hand of God? Did the Germans simply out-pray us?

A boat drops its ramp, the soldiers start out, and they fall before they hit the water. Arms flailing, hands vainly in front of their faces trying to stop the onslaught of bullets. I am dying with them. There is cursing around me. Men grunt and snort. We are becoming animals, trapped, fearful, wanting to live.

More of the men coming in make it to the beach. I see the ships have come closer, their guns roaring, pounding the cliffs. The noise is deafening. It fills me up and takes away anything that is sane in me.

I will never be the same again. I am new. And ugly. And fearful. But I will never be the same again.

We Might Die Here

"We're going to die here!" A voice to my left. I turned and saw a guy I once played softball with. His face was bandaged and there was something dark oozing from his nose and mouth. "We're going to die here!"

"If we're going to die, then we're going to die up on the hill, soldier!" An officer, tall, angular, a .45 in his hand. "Get ready to move out!"

"I don't have a rifle, sir," I said.

The officer looked at me, looked at the rifle I still held, and then looked away. Suddenly he stood, walked out on the sand, and picked up a rifle next to a dead body. He brought it back to where I still sat and handed it to me.

"Now you got one!" he said.

I glanced at the body that had once held the rifle I now held. *Poor bastard,* I thought. He never even had a chance to use it.

"The draw is to the right, thirty yards," the officer said. "We'll move to it and figure a way to get up where the Germans are waiting for us. Let's go!"

He crouched low and started toward the draw. Nothing in me wanted to move, but somehow I knew I had to follow him. I got to my feet and tried to close the gap between us. Behind me another shell hit in front of the area where some of the men still crouched. I turned once more to the beach and noticed, for the first time, that none of the bodies were together. Like good soldiers, they hadn't bunched.

The draw widened at the bottom and was exposed. On the far right side there were several small fires. They poured black smoke. Rubber or fuel. I couldn't see through the smoke, but I welcomed it. It was something between me and the enemy.

I hadn't yet seen my first live German. The dead and wounded, twisted and still on the wet sand, said that they were there. We had run onto a great invisible death machine. It was looking for more victims.

"If they send a company down the draw they'll wipe us out in minutes!" someone was saying. It was the man who had picked up a rifle for me. "If we're going to die, we'll die up there fighting, not down here hiding!"

A ranger, crawling on his belly, went a few yards up the draw. I saw his body jerk from the force of the bullets ripping into him. He turned over slowly until he faced the sky, only to have more bullets hit him. A feeling of nausea came over me.

The draw was nothing more than a wide road. It was easy to imagine families making their way from the town. Their arms would be filled with baskets of food, bottles of wine and soda. They would have blankets to lay on the sand.

But now, June 6, 1944, thirty feet up, perhaps higher, it was not a place for families. There was an ugly roll of barbed wire at least four feet high above us. The roll was thicker than the wire we had climbed through in the water and ran the width of the draw. Cutting through the wire would mean standing still for precious seconds in front of it. Standing for those seconds would mean certain death. The Germans knew what we would have to do to defeat them. They were waiting for us.

Two men came toward us, one hauling a bangalore torpedo.

Bangalore torpedoes took too long to set up. They could blast a path through barbed wire, but whoever placed them would be exposed to enemy fire. Everybody knew that. Everybody.

"When they start up we need to lay down some covering fire!" the officer who had given me the rifle said crisply.

"It won't work!" I heard myself saying. "They'll be —"

"They'll make it work!" the officer said.

I looked at him to see if he was serious. He was. I looked at his name tag: COTA.

It won't work! I said to myself.

A bangalore torpedo is just a tube filled with explosives. You put it under an obstacle or over antipersonnel mines and the explosion it creates will clear the obstacles or detonate the mines. But you have to place it just right. I knew the Germans had their guns ready to kill any man who tried it, as they had killed the ranger.

A minute — no, seconds — later, a short soldier ran up the draw, the bangalore torpedo like a stiff snake at his side. He fell forward as the first bullets hit him, then pushed himself to his knees and twisted as the second blast ripped through him.

He rolled backward, hands beating the cold, damp air above his head. Before he had stopped moving, before his already dead body had stopped twitching, another soldier had already grabbed the bangalore. Had pushed it forward. I saw him grabbing his legs as he was hit. I saw him spin away from the torpedo, and then saw it go off in a great cloud of smoke and debris.

"Let's go! Let's go!" Cota was on his feet and starting up the draw.

Somehow I was moving, running as hard as I could up the draw. There were men to my left and my right. I was glad I wasn't alone.

Phut! Phut! Phut!

"Oh my God!" The man on my right stumbled forward, his body twisting as he went down, his arms reaching up.

I kept running. We were past the barbed wire, and now there were trees and boulders. Some of the men got behind the boulders and started shooting in the direction where they thought the Germans were. Others kept going forward toward a two-story building.

"Aim for the slits!" someone yelled. "They're shooting from the slits!"

What were they talking about? What the hell were they talking about? There was a ditch, maybe six feet across and twice that distance deep. I tried to jump it and didn't make it across, sliding down, clutching at dirt and rocks until I finally stopped. Then I scratched my way up as others half flung, half scrambled their way across the ditch.

At ground level I brought my rifle up and looked to find something to shoot at.

On the hill to my right I saw what looked like a mound of bricks and concrete, but it had dark spaces, and I knew those were the slits from which the deadly fire was coming.

I got the M1 to my shoulder and aimed at the first dark spot I saw. The kick from the rifle felt good. I didn't see anybody, I didn't know if anybody was still behind those slits, but at least I was fighting back. At least I was fighting back.

Without turning my head I could feel the guys who had come off the beach running around me. The changes in their voices, from desperation to sharply barked commands, meant that we were a fighting force again; we were soldiers instead of lambs being led to the slaughter.

I felt a hand touch my shoulder and jumped.

"Good work," a voice said. "Let's move into the town. We need to clear it out. Work with any officer you find to set up a perimeter. What's your MOS?"

"Infantry, sir. The 29th."

"Good, keep up the good work!"

The men coming up the draw weren't running anymore. Now they were moving quickly, confidently. None of us knew who we were with at that time, but we moved into the small city. I remembered its name, Vierville-sur-Mer, knowing that I would never forget it.

Confused, tired, I moved into the town. Soldiers I had never seen before were all around me. A lot of them wore 29th patches; some were First Army.

An old woman, thin, tall, stood in front of what remained of a white building. Her shoulders moved up and down as if she was crying somewhere within the fragile shell of her being. Waving a pale hand to us as we approached her, she tried to speak and couldn't. Getting closer to her, I could see her tear-streaked face. Her eyes darted from soldier to soldier as if she was wondering who we were. As if she was wondering *what* we were.

Officers grabbed men as we went by. A short major called me over, asked what outfit I was in, and told me to fall in with him.

"I've got the eastern perimeter," he said. "We'll dig in on the edge of town for the night. You got that?"

"Yeah."

"What?"

"Yeah, sir," I said.

"No, I mean do you really understand what I'm saying?"

"I think I do," I said. "We have to do something on the east. Then we'll move on."

"How old are you, son?"

"Nineteen, sir."

"That's a good age," the officer said. "That's a damn good age."

He ran ahead of me and I followed him the best I could. My legs were going in every direction and I was moving, but nothing made sense. There were guys lying on the road and just off of it. Some were wounded and others already dead.

Inside my head the noises got louder, and I felt myself crying inside. All of a sudden I was five again and lost and scared. Five again and lost and scared. Lost and scared.

A Small Company of Men

"We're the 29th, we're damned good, and we're going to keep on fighting!"

Lieutenant Milton didn't look like a soldier to me. More like a car salesman, or somebody who sold feed. But we had been gathered and told that he was in charge of us.

"Anybody got any questions?"

"What company are we with?" Gomez asked. "It's all mixed up."

"Yeah, and so we're now a fighting *unit* until we get it straightened up," Milton said. "We're going to start talking to one another, and living with one another, and looking out for one another. I want each of you to introduce yourselves so that we're people. Not just serial numbers, but people. You can start, Gomez."

"What you want me to say?"

"Tell everybody who you are," Milton said. "That'll be a start."

"Why I got to start?"

"Because I said so," Milton answered.

"Shit!" Gomez looked away. "So my family came to the States in 1924. In the States things weren't that good for them but it was better than what they had in Mexico. So they came. I don't remember much of that because I was too friggin' young.

"We lived in Roanoke and it was okay. I didn't join the National Guard because my dad wouldn't let me. But when the war broke out, I joined up because I'm an American and I thought it was my duty. I didn't know nothing about this stuff."

"What stuff?" Milton asked.

"Guys being killed like what happened on the beach," Gomez said. "I didn't see it like that. I just seen it like I had a job to do, like we all had a job to do, and I joined up. There's nothing fancy about me. I don't have any deep thoughts about anything. I'm more like the kids who fought at Chapultepec. That was a war the Americans had against my people. In the history books it was kind of heroic. Maybe I should have thought more. I don't know. But I'm an American, not a Mexican, and for me it was my country at war, so it was my fight."

"Next." Milton pointed toward Shumann.

"Arnold Shumann, Baltimore. First, I wanted to kill Japs. That was right after Pearl Harbor," Shumann said. "Then, when they sent me to Iceland and then to England, I wanted to kill Germans. You mess with me and I mess with you. That's how I go. We come over here and all these guys end up dying in the water and on the sand and I want to kill a whole bunch of people. I hate them. But even if I didn't hate them I would want to kill them. I was made to be a soldier.

"My dad thought I should have been a factory worker, like he was. He made farm machinery. Once a year he took us all up to Richmond for a vacation. I hate Richmond. I never met anybody from Richmond I ever liked in my whole life.

"That's pretty much me. After what I seen here, I want to kill Germans more than anything I ever wanted. If they kill me it don't even matter, because God gave me a friggin' chance to kill them."

"Burns?"

"I was drafted. Didn't care much about Germans or Japs. I don't like any of them. I don't like Negroes, either. Nothing personal. I just don't like people who are different from me. Everybody in this group is like a brother to me. I'll fight for them. If there was a German or a Jap or a Negro in this group, I would fight for them. I think I'm pretty good.

"I never thought much of dying. Maybe I should have. I don't know. When I saw all those guys out there — lying out there — I felt like shit. I wanted to give them something. Maybe some payback. But dying never meant nothing to me until I saw those guys out there. I guess it should have meant something. Right now I'm appreciating stuff I never held too high before. Like pan bread.

"Back home my mother used to make pan bread when I was a kid and I didn't like it. You know what pan bread is? You make it on top of the stove with flour and water and a half cake of yeast, and an egg if you got one. Then you cook it up. I hated pan bread because all my friends got bread from the grocery store or the bakery.

"Right now, I don't give a damn about anything except moving my ass along the map across France and into Germany. I'm thinking more about dying now that I seen so many men die. I'm thinking more about how I'm going to deal with it. In a way I hope I go out good. Not smiling or nothing, but going out good, going out trying to get the job done. Wish I had done more thinking on all of this a long time ago. I didn't, so that's that."

"Woody?" Milton looked at me. "What are you making of all this?"

I didn't know what he meant at first. Why was I talking about who I was when half the world I knew had just died? How was I going to know about who I was?

I looked over at Gomez and I was glad to see him. I was glad to see his hair coming down into his face and his dark pretty eyes still open.

"Wedgewood!" Lieutenant Milton said.

"I'm from Bedford, Virginia. Bedford's a good place to live. Small town, good people," I said. "I was pretty much raised in the church and even thought I might like to go into a seminary. But I'm good at art, too. And I saw that not that many people can draw as well as I can, or even see the beauty in things the way I do. So I went up to New York to art school. It was a way of getting away from home, too. When the war broke out and my mom wrote to me that they were calling up the 29th, I went home and enlisted. I'm confused about this fighting and, like the others said, about people dying so fast. I just hope I get it figured out before . . . you know, something happens to me."

"Why don't you go, sir?" Gomez said to Lieutenant Milton.

"I'm from Glenarden, Maryland." Lieutenant Milton spoke slowly. "I'm not into glory or being brave or even killing anybody. The country was attacked, and I took a look at my life and saw it wasn't amounting to much, and it wasn't going anywhere in particular because it didn't *have* to go anywhere. My family has money. We own a small store in Washington and two up in New York. My dad knew how to make money, still does. He offered to buy my way out of the war, and he could have done it, too.

"I didn't want any part of that, and not too much more of him, either. He did pull some strings and I got a gold bar instead of a PFC stripe. I hope to make a good soldier. Other than that I'm just like everybody else."

"This don't sound like much of an outfit," Stagg said. "But it'll do."

Silence.

"So what's your story, Stagg?" Lieutenant Milton asked.

"No story," he answered. "I'm here, I'll carry my load."

"Minkowitz?"

"Amherst, philosophy major," he said. "My parents are divorced. My mom lives in New York. She doesn't think I'll make it back. I'm not sure, either. I hope . . . I hope I carry my load."

"You tell your dad you joined?"

"Yeah, he asked me if I had insurance," Minkowitz said.

"Freihofer?"

"This is stupid." Freihofer spoke through clenched teeth. "It has no meaning. What difference does it make where you are from or what your parents are doing? I don't care if you make bread in a pan or in an oven. All this is bullshit. We are not here to love one another or take care of one another. We are here like ants who are supposed to crawl around on a big map and capture towns. If we don't capture the towns, then they will send more ants. None of this talk will help us. It didn't help any of those poor bastards lying in the sand. You know we are only ten minutes away from the water? You know that if we are attacked now most of us don't even have rifles to shoot back? Don't give me your bullshit, soldier."

"Freihofer? Is that German?" Petrocelli said.

"It's as German as Adolf Hitler," Freihofer snarled.

"You speak German?" Lieutenant Milton asked.

"What difference does it make?"

"It might make a difference somewhere down the line, Freihofer, and I want to know now," Lieutenant Milton said. "And I don't care if you think this is bullshit or not! If you give me any more lip, I'll shoot you myself!"

"I speak German," Freihofer said.

"Scott?"

"My friends call me Scotty," Scott said. "I was working in a garage when we got called up. I don't have a story, really. I'm just a working guy who gets along with everybody, more or less. I'm not the hero type, but I don't run from a fight, either."

Lyman couldn't talk. He kept trying, kept opening his mouth, but nothing came out. I thought he was going to break down, but then Lieutenant Milton patted him on the knee and pointed to Petrocelli, who said he had to go take a crap. When he got up to go, Mac went with him. I hadn't heard him speak, and guessed he wasn't up to it now. I wished I hadn't said anything.

Milton looked pissed. I knew he was trying to get us together again as a fighting unit, and some of the guys were buying it. What we had to do, what we were trying to figure out, was who the hell we were. Sometimes you come up with words and they don't mean a lot. Like, it didn't matter if I was raised in Bedford, or if I went to art school. I wasn't even sure if it mattered if we crawled across the map of France like ants. I didn't know what mattered anymore, because the world had changed. On Tuesday, the sixth day of June, 1944, the world had stopped being what I thought it was. There were guys I had laughed with and grumbled with and even joked with about what we would be doing in Paris or Berlin, and now they were dead. I didn't know who had made it off the beach, or who had even got that far. I thought guys had drowned before they even got on shore.

And none of it was coming together for me. What I felt was desperation. Wild and nasty, and not like anything I had ever known before.

We moved into the town, into Vierville, men damned near shaking in their skins, trying to grasp what was happening. The men I was with moved around the edge of the town, behind the smoking buildings, the charred walls. *This is what combat is about. This and the killing.* As we moved, there was gunfire behind us and on the right, in the center of the town, and I imagined there were Germans hiding out, or that some had doubled back. What I knew was that there was a lot of confusion.

A bunch of us gathered with some officers and we were kind of sorted out. The ones with rifles and ammo were distributed to the few officers around, and I found myself with Lieutenant Milton again. I was glad to see him.

"They're changing plans every thirty minutes!" Lieutenant Milton said. "Now they want us to move out as quickly as possible and head in the general direction of St. Lo. That's our next big objective. What they're worried about is a major German counterattack. We captured a lot of the Krauts, but they told us that a lot got away. If they team them up with an armored division, we're in for a hell of a fight."

"Especially since we don't have any tanks," Kroll said.

"They'll bring them ashore as fast as they can," Milton went on. "But we need to set up a perimeter big enough to establish a supply base and jumping-off point. According to the first plans, we were supposed to be in St. Lo this afternoon."

"Yo, Lieutenant, did they expect any Germans to be here?" Stagg asked.

"I think they didn't expect an experienced combat outfit to be here," Milton answered. "But it doesn't matter now. We're here and we have to move before the Germans get reorganized."

"It matters to me, sir," Petrocelli said. "We were the first on the beach and we got our asses shot up. We were the first to move inland and we got our asses shot up. Now we got to get out further so when the Krauts bring up tanks they got some experienced shot-up asses to shoot at?"

"Petrocelli, I've heard just about enough of your mouth." Lieutenant Milton spoke slowly, deliberately. "If I hear any more I'm going to close it for you myself."

I watched Petrocelli's jaw tighten, relax, and tighten again. If Milton hadn't been an officer, there would have been a fight.

Milton told us to check our weapons, then stalked off. Petrocelli raised one finger and pointed at the officer as he left.

"Why don't you give it a rest, Petrocelli?" This from Mac.

"Back in Bayonne, in my cousin Alberto's restaurant, there's this old guy who used to hang around," Petrocelli said. "The guy had to be ancient. He could have been fifty, even sixty, and his neck was all wrinkled. But for an old guy, he was smart. He used to say that if something looked like a pizza, it *wanted to be* a pizza. He said that about some guys, too. If a guy looked like a bum, he *wanted* to be a bum. So, back in England, when I saw the pictures of Vierville-sur-Mer, it looked like a friggin' beach. I thought this invasion was going to be a picnic."

"A picnic?" Kroll asked. "You saying you weren't scared?"

"No, I was a little scared. Maybe more nervous than scared, but the pictures they showed us had Vierville looking like a beach, with people sitting around on the sand. I don't really trust nothing with a French name. Even when they call it a *saint* something. And I've been Catholic all my life, and I've never heard of a Saint Lo.

"Anyway, what this looks like to me is that the 29th is being put out there to find out where the Krauts are. We stick our necks out, the Krauts pick us off, and then the brass says, 'Oh, that's where they are!'"

We packed up for the move from Vierville toward Bayeux. Some of the guys were getting themselves together. I wasn't sure if I would ever be the same guy who got on the boat on the fourth, but I was calming down some.

The thing that bothered me the most was that everybody looked different. Before I had seen men with eyes and noses and ears and they looked friendly or not friendly. Now I had seen some of those same men lying on Omaha Beach, had seen them curled up and lifeless by the side of the road, had seen them with their faces blown away or blackened by fire. They didn't look like men anymore, they looked like some strange creatures you'd see in a nightmare. And their being dead didn't make any sense, because being dead was supposed to be something you did when you got old, when you were home in your bed and coughing into a handkerchief. It was, in a way, at least in my mind, something that you made peace with before it happened, that you agreed to be part of. Instead it was something that happened to you with a violence you couldn't understand, or at least I couldn't understand. I told myself I wasn't scared of dying. The words got into my head, but I couldn't even say them out loud. It was true, in a weird kind of way, that I wasn't scared of dying, but I was scared of the violence, of the suddenness that I saw get other men. They would be hit and you could see the surprise on their faces, and then the panic, and then, maybe, the knowing that they were going to die.

We got into some kind of line and started down the road to Bayeux. There were two Sherman tanks rolling in front of us. Lord, I didn't want to be in a tank. I had seen them hit, and seen the guys burning as they tried to escape. I didn't want to burn to death.

"Hey, Woody." It was Minkowitz. "You think a French city is like New York?"

"No, how come you're asking that?"

"You've been to New York," Mink said. "I bet most of these guys haven't been to New York."

"I bet Petrocelli's been to New York," I said. "I had a girl in one of my art classes who lived in Hoboken. If she could come into the city three times a week, then Petrocelli must have been in New York a hundred times."

"Yo, Gomez!" Mink called over to Gomez, who was walking near Petrocelli. "Ask Petrocelli if he's ever been to New York."

Petrocelli turned and gave Mink a look. "Yo, knucklehead, I friggin' *own* New York. Nothing happens in that city without my saying it's all right."

"Stay alert! Stay alert! There could be snipers in the city."

I knew that. I knew some German soldier could be hiding behind a tree, or in a building, drawing a bead on one of us. Maybe he had a machine gun and was just waiting for the right time to open up. Or maybe he was as scared as I was. I wondered if the others could see how I felt inside. If they knew the terror I felt.

We slow-marched four miles toward Bayeux and set up loose defenses around a small village that looked a lot like the outskirts of Bedford as it grew dark. I thought about soldiers surrounding our little city in Virginia and it made me sad. And just as in Vierville, the occasional *pop! pop!* of a rifle coming from the darkness kept us all on edge.

Lieutenant Milton kept checking the maps. There were signs around, giving the names of the places we were in, but it seemed to me that he wasn't sure of just where we were.

You could tell the difference between the sound of an M1, the American rifle, and the German guns. We knew that one of us, sometimes two or more if they caught us together, was going down when we heard the Kraut guns. The thing was that the Germans had more automatic weapons than we did. It didn't feel right trying to squeeze off a round against an enemy we couldn't see when they were spraying us with machine guns.

Stagg came over and told us to keep our heads down. "They want us to know they're still out there and still fighting," he said.

"If they stick their heads up, I'll kill them," Gomez said softly.

"Yeah, Gomez, they know that, too."

I dug a foxhole with Mink. We went down a full six feet with no problem. I wanted to be able to stand up and still have most of my body protected.

"You going to make a sump hole for grenades?" Mink asked.

"You want to hear something funny?" I asked. "I was with this guy in infantry training, and he said he would never dig out a sump hole for grenades. You know why?"

"Why?"

"You know you're supposed to dig a hole so in case somebody throws a grenade into your foxhole you can kick it into the hole so when it goes off it won't get you, right?"

"Something like that," Mink said.

"Well, he said that if anybody ever threw a grenade into his foxhole, he wouldn't spend his time trying to kick it around," I said.

"He said he'd jump out of the foxhole and take a chance fighting whoever threw it. You got to admit, it's a funny picture, two guys trying to find a grenade in the dark and kicking it into a small hole."

"It's not funny," Mink said.

"Why not?"

"Because you're scaring the crap out of me," Mink said. "That's why!"

We finished digging our foxhole, and I put in a sump hole. I didn't say anything about it to Mink, but he saw me doing it and I guessed he knew what I was doing.

Stagg came around again. He was getting to be a pain in the ass since we landed in France, but I imagined it came with the territory.

"I catch both you guys sleeping at the same time, I'm going to cut one guy's balls off and one guy's head," he said. "Think about it!"

I was up first, and Mink curled up and tried to get some sleep. I knew he was tired, and I knew he was scared. He was a nice guy, kind of smart, maybe even real smart, but the fighting was getting to him. It had either got to all of us or it was getting there. We were changing. I was changing.

I thought about praying. Back home, at the training sessions, there was an old sergeant major who used to always say that there weren't any atheists in a foxhole. I didn't know about that, but I didn't want God hearing me pray and thinking about how long it had been since I had gone to a Sunday service or even thought about him. On the other hand, I didn't want him making a list of who he was going to let live and who he was going to let die and putting my name on the wrong page.

A Company came through and asked if we had any extra rations. We gathered up what we could and gave them to a short, plump officer.

"These boys haven't had anything to eat all day, and they're dog tired," the officer was saying to Stagg. "And the brass is pushing us to go forward. What the hell are we supposed to be fighting on? Air? What the hell are we supposed to be fighting on?"

Stagg didn't answer, just nodded.

I watched as the company filed past us in the darkness. By their silhouettes you could see they were tired. I noticed some had their rifles slung upside down. I put my palm out and felt a few drops of rain.

"Stupid," Stagg said. "They're carrying M1s. They can return fire faster with the barrels up."

"Yeah."

I hadn't seen any Germans fighting against us, or even any not fighting, except the ones who had been taken prisoner on the day of the invasion and the ones who had been captured near Vierville. And the dead ones.

As much as seeing dead Americans spooked me, especially if they wore the blue-and-gray patch of the 29th, the dead Germans spooked me even more. I didn't know why at first, but then Petrocelli nailed it.

"They're either kids, old men, or models," he said. "If they came to Bayonne we'd make them wear dresses!"

Some of the dead Germans were from the 352nd, the same guys who were in the pillboxes on the beach. These guys were all tall, well built. Even being dead they just seemed relaxed, sleeping. Milton searched them for material to send back to Intelligence. One of them, a soldier named Rudolf Mallner, carried a mass card for his brother, who had been killed on the eastern front. The back of the mass card had two images of Jesus, one on the cross and the other with the crown of thorns.

I Am Thinking Back, Not Forward

My balls were itching like crazy a mile into the march south, and I realized I hadn't taken a real bath or even done much washing since I had landed in France. I ignored it. I didn't want to think about anything. That's a funny way to be, but it's how I was getting — just sort of zoning out — and my mind drifted back toward me enlisting.

There had been no direct bus from New York City to Bedford, Virginia, so I took a late afternoon bus from the Port Authority building to Roanoke, and planned to either hitchhike or find a bus going from Roanoke to get home. All the way down I thought about joining the Army and what I would do. I had never wanted to be a hero, and stopped myself when I thought about fighting hand-to-hand battles with the Japs or doing anything heroic against the Germans. But I wanted to do my part. Pearl Harbor had been attacked and over two thousand Americans had been killed. President Roosevelt had called it a day that would live in infamy. And when Hitler declared war on us a few days later, I knew we were going to be in for something big.

All the training at Slapton Sands, England, made me feel good, and patriotic. I knew we were training to liberate Europe, and I knew we could do it. Somebody beating America just wasn't in my mind. I liked the English girls looking at us and maybe wondering if we were going to save the world. I thought we were going to do just that, but what happened on the beach changed everything.

It wasn't that I didn't want to do my part anymore, because I did. But all the guys killed on Omaha, all the guys struggling with their last breaths trying to make it out of the water, brought a whole new picture to mind, and a whole new feeling. Now I was always dog tired, tired like I had never been before in my life, and I knew a few hours of sleeping wasn't going to change that. It was like whatever something was in me — the something that made me different from a rock or a fence or a photograph on a wall — was gone. I found myself telling my legs to move when I wanted to walk and telling myself to swallow when I ate. Sleep didn't come easy, and when it did it was full of images, like an old newsreel playing back what had happened during the landing.

There were sounds, too. Sometimes when I woke in the middle of the night, I could hear the sounds of the channel slapping against the sides of the boat and the roar of the engines as we bounced through the water. The cries of grown men crying for their mamas and for God came in between the sounds of the water and the booming of the big guns.

I couldn't tell the difference between our artillery and the German artillery at first. I didn't know if the Germans had guns as big as ours or what they sounded like. I did know the sounds of machine gun bullets hitting close by, or tearing down the limbs of a tree I huddled under. I knew the burping noise their guns made, and the quick tattoo when their bullets hit flesh. I knew that.

We stopped to rest. Mink came over and sat next to me. We were becoming friends. No big deal talk, no arms around each other, just friends.

Mink asked me if I was afraid. He didn't say afraid of this or that, just asked me if I was afraid. I lied and said no. It wasn't the answer he was looking for, I knew. I didn't want to tell him just how afraid I was, or how sometimes, when I was alone, I wanted to break down and cry.

Some brass came by. They told us to get ready to move on. Milton — we were beginning to appreciate him — sat down with us and showed us a map. A dot was circled in red marker.

"We're going to take this area," he said.

"We don't have enough ammo to beat a den of Cub Scouts," Stagg said.

"Then you better have your bayonet sharpened!" Milton said softly.

Stagg had put himself out, talking like that to an officer, but it didn't make a difference. At 0400 hours in the morning, we were moving again.

We are moving back toward Omaha Beach. The word is that we are forming a new offensive line. The Germans are moving up reserves and we will be attacking them. Lieutenant Milton thinks that we are just seeing "what the Germans can muster up in a hurry." He tried to smile when he said it but I think he's losing his nerve. Lord knows I've lost mine.

This time we got on trucks behind two small tracked vehicles and started out. It was six miles to Longueville, where some companies from the 175th were setting up. It was good to see their pennant, and their guys didn't look too banged up. We had to get out of the trucks and go the rest of the way on foot.

"I think the Germans have bugged out," Shumann said. "We got our feet on the ground; it's just about over for them!"

I felt good about that even though there was no reason to really believe it. Then a jeep came up with a colonel in it. I was near Milton when he gave him the latest news.

"Vierville was attacked. The Germans have circled around us," he said.

"We going back?" Milton asked.

"No, you're moving forward to keep the Krauts occupied in this area," the colonel said. "Same objective. We need to keep them spread out so they can't form up for a counterattack. It's all cat and mouse, so keep your eyes open."

Lieutenant Milton threw the colonel a salute and looked at us. I could tell he wasn't happy with the situation. I thought about what Petrocelli had said about the 29th being used to find the enemy. I guessed we all must have felt that way.

The Army was filled with scuttlebutt, the rumors that spread from man to man and from company to company. Half the time they weren't true, but that didn't stop everyone from wondering about each new one. Now the rumor was that the brass thought we weren't moving fast enough, that we were giving the Krauts a chance to recover. I looked around me at the guys in my squad. They were still deep into themselves, and I knew they were searching the same as I was.

We quick-marched down the road for another mile until we came to some fields. We halted, and someone — it might have been Colonel Cawthon or some other hotshot — had us spread out in a long skirmish line. Able Company, or what was being called Able Company, was out front, with us a hundred yards behind them. There was a row of trees and we had to go through them, across a field, and then past a second row of trees. Lieutenant Milton called Burns and Stagg over and showed them a map. He was near me, so I took a step over and looked to see what they were talking about.

"These are the hedgerows," he said, pointing to the green markings on the map. "The French farmers use them to separate their fields."

"They look like little flower patches on the fucking map," Burns said.

I looked at Lieutenant Milton to see what he would say to Burns about his language. He was biting his lip and shaking his head. "We got our pictures from the air," he said. "This is the real deal, and I've got a bad feeling about crossing these fields."

"Why?" I asked.

"Because we got to cross this flat-ass field, and we can't see what's past the other hedgerows," Lieutenant Milton said. "And you're going to be halfway across before we find out."

"When we moving out?" Burns asked.

"We'll get a signal when Able Company makes contact," Lieutenant Milton said.

"In other words, we don't know what the hell we're doing," Burns said.

"Sergeant, we know we're fighting a war, and we know we're catching hell," Lieutenant Milton said. "If you have a better plan let's hear it!"

Burns turned and spit on the ground.

We spread out along the nearest hedgerow. The hedgerow wasn't like anything we would call a hedgerow back in Virginia. They were tall, some over six feet tall, with trees and bushes on them that sent roots as thick as my arm through the dark soil. You couldn't see over them and you couldn't see what was behind the next one.

"This does not look good," Freihofer said. "We got to run

blind across the field and hope that the Krauts aren't just waiting for us!"

It's what we've been doing since we've been over here, I thought. We came out of the boats and waded toward the beach while the Germans waited for and killed as many of us as they could. They were waiting for us in Vierville, and along the roads, and now they had circled around and attacked again at Vierville. What had happened to all the dumb Germans we had joked about in training?

The sky was gray, with a streak of light off to the south where the clouds broke. I couldn't see Able Company for a while, and then I started seeing outlines of their helmets as they moved across the field.

"Able Company's moving out now," Milton said. "Let's hit our positions behind this hedgerow and cover them. Don't bunch up!"

The M1 I was carrying felt light in my hands, but I hadn't been using it and realized that it might not have been zeroed in for a hundred yards, which was about what the field was. I took a quick look at the sights, saw that they were more or less centered, and climbed onto the edge of the first hedgerow. Shumann was on my right and Petrocelli was on my left.

The hedgerow was as tall as me, with bushes and shrubs and low trees that had probably been growing there for fifty years. Able Company guys had climbed through them and then lowered themselves the four feet or so to the field. The field looked good. It smelled a little like barley, but I couldn't tell for sure.

What was supposed to happen was that Able Company was supposed to establish themselves at the first hedgerow across the field, and then we were supposed to follow them, go through their position, and make our way to the next hedgerow. Then Charlie Company would follow us and we'd leapfrog until we cleared enough ground to think the whole area was safe.

"Woody! What're you thinking about?" This from Shumann.

"Mom's apple pie!" I said. What the hell was I supposed to be thinking? "What are you thinking about?"

"I'm thinking that if Able Company gets into a firefight, how are we going to help them out if we have to shoot in their direction?"

"We'll call in mortars!" Petrocelli called out. "Maybe some artillery. Right, Woody?"

"Yeah," I said. Shumann was right, but I wished he hadn't brought it up.

I turned my attention back to the field. Able Company was halfway across and it looked good. The palms of my hands were sweating, and I wiped my right hand off on my pants leg.

"Baker Company, get ready to move out!" Lieutenant Milton barked.

I was lying next to a thick shrub stump and got up to one knee just as we heard the first shots.

I looked up and saw a line of guys from Able Company reel backward as they got hit. There were machine guns hidden in the hedgerows, and they opened up and mowed down a line of guys.

The Able Company men didn't know what to do. It was the beach all over again: men out in the open facing German machine guns. I wanted to do something, anything, but I didn't know what. Some of the men from Able Company were down in the prone position, firing at the hedgerows. I looked but I couldn't see anybody shooting at them, only the occasional muzzle flash from a German machine gun.

I heard someone calling in coordinates for mortar fire, and in seconds the sounds of the shells from the mortar squads were in the air.

"Fire at the trees, just keep it up!" Lieutenant Milton yelled. "Keep it high enough not to hit our men."

We all began firing. It was blind fire, and we knew it. The men in the field were either down and firing back or trying to run back to our lines. The ones who stood, who tried to run, were being taken down.

The firing lasted less than five minutes and then stopped. I could see some of the men from Able Company throwing grenades toward the hedgerows. To my right the grass and shrubbery was on fire.

"Cease fire! Cease fire!"

Medics were running out onto the field, and some of the men from Baker Company were already moving out.

"Let's go! Let's go!" Lieutenant Milton said.

Dying in the Hedgerows

I was shaking as I climbed through the hedgerow, scraping the skin off my forearm, and let myself down onto the field.

"Stay low! Stay low!" Lieutenant Milton said.

We moved in a line across the field with Lieutenant Milton yelling instructions to us. I was holding my breath as I ran forward, my eyes shooting from side to side, looking for the machine guns, waiting for the burping noise they made, waiting for the feel of the bullets.

We got to the Able Company men. Three were already dead, and at least six lay wounded in the thick, green field. Several others were wounded but still on their feet or sitting up on the ground.

"Hold it! Get prone!" Sergeant Burns said. "Lieutenant, you call a cease-fire for the mortars?"

Lieutenant Milton got on the radio. He called for a cease-fire, but said for the mortar crews to stand ready. Then he stood up and started for the hedgerows again.

My legs didn't want to work; they didn't want to run anywhere. Somehow they did. We got to the rows. The Germans had fallen back again. They left two behind. One was dead, his helmet ripped open on the left side. The other one was wounded in the jaw. His mouth was open and bleeding, and he couldn't close it.

Stagg started searching him. He took papers out of his vest pocket, what ammo he had left, and a dagger from his belt. All the time the soldier was bleeding from the mouth and shaking in fear. His eyes kept darting around, and I knew he was wondering if we would kill him. He probably couldn't speak any English, but he was begging with his eyes.

"Look out for mines!" Burns barked.

We dug in behind the hedgerow. The next row was about twice the width of the one we had just crossed. Lieutenant Milton was already calling in the coordinates for the mortar squad.

"Either they're setting up and waiting for us," he said, "or they've moved beyond that one. As soon as the mortars zero in on the hedges ahead of us, we'll move out."

The mortars started hitting short of the rows, and Stagg radioed the distance. We watched as they began to hit their targets and got up and started across the open field.

There were a few shots fired at us, and I saw a man go down to my left. If anybody stopped and turned back, I knew I would, too. But

Milton kept going forward, and Stagg was close to him. We got across the field to the next hedgerow with no more casualties.

The Germans had fired a few shots but hadn't stopped to set up a line of defense.

"We lost one man!" A skinny corporal came over to where we were. He wore the arm patch of a medic. "Anybody hit here?"

No one spoke up.

"What they're doing is fighting a delaying action!" Milton said. "They're trying to slow us down across the hedgerows while they bring up reinforcements. The plan for us is *not* to slow down, to keep them moving backward faster than they can set up a defensive wall."

We set up again and waited for the mortars to clear the next hedgerows. We examined the one we were at and saw that there were narrow holes dug through the base of the rows, with rocks lining them to keep the dirt from falling in. They were just wide enough for a machine gun to have room to sweep the field. The Krauts had made the holes long before the invasion. They knew we were coming and had marked off the killing fields that we were trying to cross.

In basic we were always talking about the Germans as if they were stupid. We called them Krauts and Jerries, as if they weren't really people like us. But up close we could see that they had planned as much as we had, had thought about the invasion as much as we had, and were ready for us to come. It was a scary feeling.

I looked out through the thick shrubbery toward the next line. It was short, maybe seventy yards. If we ran fast enough, we could get across it in ten seconds. If the Germans were set up there, they could kill half the company in that ten seconds.

"It's like fighting with a blindfold on," Petrocelli said. "You run across the field toward a row and hope that some Kraut son of a bitch doesn't have you in his sights. Then, if you make it over, you got to kill him hand to hand, and he don't give a damn because he's fighting for Hitler, and they all love *Der Führer*."

I didn't know why the Germans were fighting, but I knew they were killing and wounding a lot of Americans. And when we were training we had somehow, in our minds, made them into stupid, goose-stepping fools. Now we saw they weren't.

We relaxed where we were and called in mortar fire against the next hedgerow. Behind us we saw Charlie Company moving forward. They would have to take their chances sprinting across the field.

"Woody, how much is 240 divided by 23?" Mink asked me.

"How much is . . . ?" I tried to figure it out, but couldn't. "A little less than ten. Something near ten. I don't know, why?"

"Because I figure we're losing one man every ten yards across these fields," Mink said. "That's what it's costing us."

"Fuck you!" I said.

I liked Mink. He was quiet, thoughtful. If we had met in civilian life I would have hung out with him. But there were things I didn't want to know, that I didn't want to think about. One of them was anything that reminded me of how cheap my life had become.

"Hey, Mink, I'm sorry," I said.

"Yeah," he answered. "Me too."

Charlie Company came up, but their commanding officer didn't have them go forward as a company. Instead he sent a patrol around the edge of the field.

We watched as the seven guys on patrol edged their way down one side of the field, keeping as low as they could and running in single file. Halfway across the field, the first guy got hit by a sniper. His helmet flew off as he grabbed his head and fell forward.

"Sniper in the trees!" Petrocelli yelled.

We lit up the trees, the bullets chopping away at the branches, until someone yelled, "Cease fire!"

The patrol got up and another man was hit. He fell to his knees, crossed his arms across his chest, and slumped forward.

The rest of the patrol backed off and headed back to where we were as we let out a barrage into the hedgerow. Some more mortars hit just beyond the field.

Dog Company moved up. I saw a group of officers getting together, and I thought they were deciding our next move. I looked at my watch, and it was 0910, ten minutes past nine. Back home in Bedford, it would still be the middle of the night. The mothers of the two men hit would be asleep, perhaps dreaming.

We dug in just in time to find some shelter from the incoming artillery. The Germans were accurate with their fire, but they weren't producing too many casualties because we were dug in deep enough to avoid getting hit with shrapnel unless it exploded almost on top of us. But whenever a shell hit, the ground shook and the smell of the rounds filled the air. There was return fire from our artillery, and after about twenty minutes everything quieted down.

Some cooks showed up with cans of hot food.

"What is this?" Mink asked one of them.

The cook was dressed in fatigues that went loosely over his boots. He looked down at the food, then put his face really close to it before looking up again.

"Chicken stew?" he said — more a question than an answer.

It was some kind of brown sauce with green beans floating in it. It was delicious. I couldn't believe it was so good.

We each got a canteen of water and enough water in our mess kits to wipe them out. I didn't ask for more food, but I wished I had. Then they served coffee with instant milk packs, and that wasn't that bad.

"When I get home, I'm going to kiss my mom a thousand times every time she makes supper," Gomez said.

I hoped I would see my mom again.

Stagg and Burns went on a scouting trip to the rear and came back in a jeep with ammunition, sulfur, and bandages, which they had "borrowed."

I knew either Charlie or Dog Company was going to take the next hedgerow, so I relaxed a little. Mink came over and sat next to me.

"I'm sorry about what I said earlier," he said. "I was just nervous."

"No problem," I answered. "We're all nervous."

"Not like me," Mink answered. "I'm scared out of my mind. . . . I'm sorry I said that."

I didn't answer him. I knew he was struggling with what was going on in his head. I was struggling to keep it out of my head. I didn't want to think about anything.

Some guys from First Army came up with a group of civilians. They had good-fitting uniforms, and I wondered if they had had them cut down. A lot of guys did that back in the States. They said that the guys who were with them were prisoners — Germans who had switched into civilian clothing. They brought two of them over to where Milton and Cawthon were meeting, and Stagg sat in on their conference. Afterward, Stagg told us what he had heard.

"These guys were captured this morning and they think they might be with German Intelligence," he said. "Since they found them in civilian clothing, they can just shoot them."

"How did they know they were soldiers?" Mink asked.

"The Frenchies pointed them out," Stagg said. "They speak good French and English. They're talking their heads off so we don't hand them over to the French Resistance."

"They'll kill them?" I asked.

"Probably torture them first," Stagg said. "Then kill them."

"Is that right?" Shumann asked. "To torture or kill a prisoner of war?"

"You take your uniform off and you're not a prisoner of war," Stagg said. "You're a spy. And out here, does anyone really give a damn about what's right and what's nice? Do you really give a damn, Shumann?"

Shumann's question surprised me, but it made sense. He had wanted to kill everybody until he got into the war himself. Now he was thinking about the rules. There were a lot of questions we were asking ourselves — or at least I was asking myself — that we didn't want to answer. The next one came really fast.

Charlie Company's commanding officer got relieved of duty. He was told to take off his captain's bars and report to battalion head-quarters. A private was being sent back with him. The private, his leg in bandages, was blindfolded, and his hands were tied behind his back.

"What happened?" Petrocelli asked.

"He was supposed to take his company across the hedgerow and he didn't," Lieutenant Milton said of the commanding officer. "He decided that it was too costly and disobeyed a direct order. The private shot himself in the ankle."

"What's going to happen to him?" I asked.

"They may give him a summary court-martial and then shoot him," Lieutenant Milton answered.

I looked over at Mink, and he looked away. We both knew that we would all pay a price across these hedgerows. What we didn't know was how personal it was going to get.

I tried thinking about home, but it kept slipping away from me. What I was hoping for was something good to fill my head, maybe a picture of Mom on the porch peeling vegetables or Dad trying to fix the old generator that never worked for more than ten minutes at a time. But all I could get was the idea of the soldier blindfolded, his hands tied behind his back, and the captain going back. That and Mink's numbers.

"Hey, Mink, where did you get those numbers?" I asked.

"Figured how many yards we've crossed and how many men have gone down so far," he said.

Gone down. That's what it was about, the killing. We ran across the fields and they killed us, or we killed them, and then we got to the next field and did it again. Maybe we had more men to offer up than they did. But they knew the hedgerows, knew where the holes were to shoot through. We were just supplying the bodies.

The truth was that I wasn't seeing that many dead Germans, and even fewer wounded ones. I was getting the feeling that we were moving toward them, but they were winning. The guy who shot himself must have known the same thing. What the hell did it take to shoot yourself in the leg? How scared did you have to be? How long would it be before I got there?

A company from the 175th moved through us and started across the fields. We gave them five minutes and then followed them. It looked like they had all made it, and that made me feel good. If you followed another company, the chances were good that the Germans had already left. It was just when you were the company taking the field that you had to worry.

A couple of mortar rounds fell short, and Burns said that it probably meant that the Germans were already on the move. I didn't know about that. Everyone was guessing all the time. The thing you didn't have to guess at was that there were Germans out there waiting, and it was you they were waiting for.

A horse came onto the field in front of us. It looked slow, ponderous. It was thick-necked, the kind of working horse we had in Virginia, but with shorter legs. It looked almost like a mule. We watched as it went, seemingly without a care for all the men it had to see crouched along the hedgerows, the two small medics looking after a guy lying in the field.

"Hey, Mink, you think horses think?"

"No, they don't have language," Mink answered. "You have to have language to think in any coherent manner. He just remembers that he comes to this field."

"If he did think, what would it be about?" I asked. "I mean, if he had language."

"He'd be thinking that it isn't his freaking war and he doesn't give a damn who gets killed and who doesn't," Mink said.

Time for us to move up again. We formed a line close to the hedges, got ready, and went through. Nothing, then a few shots off to our left.

"Keep going!"

As I ran I scanned the rows for dark spots in the hedgerows that might be machine-gun nests waiting to kill us. I saw one and veered off to my right. Stagg was to my right and shot me a look. I straightened up and moved ahead.

No return fire. I was breathing again. My M1 felt light in my hand, and I was sure we were going to get to the next hedgerow all right.

"Grenades!"

I was reaching for the grenade that was fastened to my cartridge belt when I saw that there were grenades coming toward us. I hit the ground and flattened out just as the first grenade landed less than ten feet from me.

I didn't want to close my eyes or curl into a ball, but I did.

The grenade didn't go off, but the rifle fire that followed it hit the ground next to me. I looked up and saw two silhouettes standing on the hedges ahead of us, firing down at us.

Some of the other guys in the company were already returning fire when I got my rifle up. There was no aiming, just shooting in the direction of the hedges. The figures on top of the hedges were gone, and I shot at dark spots that could have been holes.

"Move out!" Lieutenant Milton yelled.

I didn't want to move anywhere, but somehow got to my feet. I looked at the grenade, jumped over it, and ran forward.

As I got to the hedgerow, I did see an opening for a rifle or machine gun. I shot through it and then climbed up the hedgerow.

I found a thick tree branch and looked over. There were three bodies lying on the ground.

Burns went over and examined the Germans to make sure they were dead. They were. Then he came back to our side of the hedge.

"Thank God their grenades didn't go off," somebody said.

"They're dummy grenades," Stagg said. "The kind they use in training. They've got to be as low on ammunition as we are. Probably lower. They just wanted to get us prone on the ground so we'd make good targets."

They had wounded five guys. Two looked like they might not make it. One man — he looked old from where I was crouched against the hedgerow — was banging the flat of his hand against the ground and tossing his head from side to side. The medic with him was trying to calm him down, and then just walked away from him.

Milton posted me and Gomez as lookouts on the left and two other guys on the right.

"You think those guys are smarter than us?" Gomez nodded to the three bodies being searched. "I mean, when they threw those grenades, I thought it was all over."

"I don't know if they're smarter," I said. "I think we're pretty smart, maybe smarter than them."

I didn't know that or even think it much. What I did know was that, standing up as they did, they were ready to die.

Some fighter planes came by and wagged their wings at us. I liked that. I was glad they recognized us and thought about what they were seeing. I wished we had had some planes back on the beach.

The five guys who were hit were taken back. Three of them had their heads covered, and I guessed they were dead.

"They threw the grenades at the guys in front to keep us down and then shot the guys coming up from the back," Gomez said, shaking his head. "And let me tell you something else."

"What?"

"I don't care if they were dummy grenades or not," Gomez said. "I'm scared of them."

All the time Gomez talked, sometimes between every two words, his tongue would come out of his mouth and he would wet his lips. I found myself doing that and knew that I was every bit as scared as he was.

A tank broke through the hedges behind us. It looked like one of our Shermans, and I was glad to see it. Petrocelli said it was about time they brought in the tanks and then started cursing out the tank crews, calling them pussies and saying that they were probably too busy whacking off in the tanks all day to do any fighting. A jeep was with the tank, and I knew it had to be Gerhardt.

"If he says anything about us not moving fast enough, I'm going to end his war myself with a bayonet up his ass!" Stagg said.

The Sherman rumbled slowly across the field. The jeep pulled around it and came barrel-assing toward our hedge. It was almost to us when the Sherman hit the mine.

■ ■ ■

Mink came over and sat near me. I knew he wanted to talk, to tell me how he felt, how afraid he was. These were things I already knew, but he was compelled to say them again. Who we were had changed in ways I never imagined. What I had always thought was that you grew from the inside, that the person you were had magically come into being as you grew and absorbed your surroundings. But what surrounded us in the weeks over there could not be absorbed. My eyes saw, my body felt, but I didn't want to see or to feel, and so I turned away.

The grass was a deep green, freshened by a light rain. In the far corner of the field behind us there was a dead cow. It lay on its side, legs stiff, stomach bloated, in a place where it had once peacefully fed. No one wanted to look at the dead animal, or squeeze it into our consciousness. It was a reminder of what our own fates could be.

Mostly it was Negroes who collected the bodies of the dead. They were in a unit called Graves Registration, which sounds better than merely collecting the dead.

A company of men started across the field. They might have been next in line to cross a field toward the next hedgerow.

"I once taught summer school in Richmond," Mink said. "I was really surprised to see how not serious the kids were."

"What grades were you teaching?" I asked.

"Sixth and seventh," he answered.

Some of the men had finished their dinners and shuffled to the three garbage cans near the mess tents. They emptied whatever was left in their mess kits into the first, then dipped the kits into the hot soapy water of the second, using the brushes on the side to clean them, and then dipped them into the clear water of the last can to get the soap off.

"I don't think they're going to shoot those guys — the captain and that soldier they took back," Mink said. "They just want to scare the crap out of us. In case we're considering running away. They're not going to shoot them, right?"

"Those guys were thinking like regular people," I said. "That's what they don't want us to do. We're supposed to run across fields with the friggin' Nazis shooting at us and not be afraid or something. I'm always wondering why I'm running at the people I don't want to see."

Mink didn't answer, just shook his head.

I watched as our company sat down against the hedgerows we were hiding behind. The sky was growing dark, and there were rain clouds blowing in our direction. I hoped the Germans were cold.

Gomez came by and gave us the thumbs-up sign. He had a small roll of toilet paper in his hand.

In the hedgerows the only place to relieve yourself with any privacy was in the occasional ruts that ran between two of the rows of gnarled trees. And then you were always afraid that some German patrol would be out looking for someone being casual, someone with his pants down or his mind in a different place. I would have loved to have found a toilet. Some place to sit and be human for a few minutes.

"Get some rest!" Milton said. "We're moving at first light! Clean your weapons if they need it."

I was beginning not to like Milton, because he always brought bad news. But he was a good man, and I felt as if he cared for us. Somebody, I think it was Stagg, said that Milton was almost twenty-six.

I put my rifle between my knees, muzzle up, and leaned against it. The smell of gunpowder and the grease from the slide mingled, but I could tell them apart as I drifted into a kind of twilight sleep.

It wasn't really a dream that came to me; it was more like a half dream, something that had been lurking in my mind for days, that I had always managed to push away, to avoid. In the dream, a group of us were sitting around having chow. It was a gray dream, and the light rain that I thought would come later in the evening had already arrived, the wind slanting the falling drops so that they found every opening, every opportunity to make life more miserable.

I glanced down into my mess kit and saw cut green beans, a lump of ground hash, and three small potatoes. When I looked up, away from the pathetic food on my plate, I saw two figures coming toward where we sat. I knew who they were before they stopped and sat. It was Sergeant Duncan and Private Kroll.

Sergeant Duncan, in life a big, square, exclamation point of a man with a wide grin and a heavy (if somewhat annoying) voice, sat heavily across from me. I looked quickly down at my plate. I was holding my breath, hoping that when I lifted my head again he wouldn't be there. I raised my eyes. He was still there, his mess kit on his lap, looking back at me.

There was no need for anyone to say that he had been killed in the cold waters off Omaha Beach, or to mention that they were sorry. Everything that needed to be said was expressed in the shadows that were his eyes. No longer the surprised agony of those final moments as he floundered desperately in the race for the sand, the life spurting from his frantic body, but, rather, the quiet darkness that we were all feeling inside, that had become part of us. I turned away again and again, but whenever I turned back to him, compelled by my own demons, his eyes would pin me to the spot.

And Kroll, the knowing laugh frozen into a chilling grimace, turning from one face to the next. Why had I pushed him out of my mind? How many more were in my mind that I had to push away, had to rid myself of? Could I move away from them even when this war was over? I didn't know. Kroll was dead. Collected by the Negroes, wrapped in canvas, and shipped home. Why?

I was accustomed to pushing thoughts from my mind. I'd grown good at it and could almost tell when a thought would come, when an image was on the verge of breaking through and filling me with an instant nightmare. Good at turning away, at avoiding those memories I didn't want to see as truths or failures, I kept myself focused on what was around me.

What was around me was Mink, trying to hold his own thoughts away from the moment, and Gomez, returning with what was left of the toilet paper, and an endless array of shadows.

What Was Home About?
Did Anyone Really Know?

Morning came, and we were issued more ammuni-tion. I watched as Burns took his gas mask out of its case and let it fall. He put the ammunition into his gas mask case. All the warnings were in place. Suppose the Krauts gassed us? Suppose we were hit with clouds of mustard gas that left us coughing our lungs out?

Burns had fought in Italy. I trusted him. I discarded my gas mask, too, and filled the case with clips. Each of us was issued twenty-five clips of ammunition, two hundred shots. The belt held ten, and I already had five clips left, so the others I put in my gas mask case. I saw Burns take a pack of cigarettes from one of his belt pouches and put them into his shirt.

I was hungry again, and thirsty. It seemed I never had enough food, but then I thought of Duncan and Kroll and the hunger went away. I made it go away and forced myself to think of Vernelle. The thought came to me that Vernelle didn't even know me and would think my letters to her ridiculous. I pushed the thought away.

Gerhardt was in the area. We saw his jeep come up and D-Day, his dog, sitting in the backseat.

Gomez stopped near me. "Hey, Woody, what do you think Uncle Charlie wants this time? You think he wants us to paint targets on our field jackets?"

"Whatever he wants, it's going to mean bad news for us," I said. "Look, he's coming this way."

We watched as Gerhardt strode over. He had a funny walk, with his legs wider than most people's. He could have been in an old cowboy movie. He stopped a few feet away from where Gomez was leaning against a tree. Gomez straightened up and snapped off a salute.

"At ease, men!" Gerhardt barked as he returned Gomez's salute. "I want those chin straps fastened and all rifles cleaned and ready for inspection at any time. Do I make myself clear?"

"Yes, sir!"

"You're going to be getting ready for a big push into St. Lo," Gerhardt went on. "The Germans have to hold it, and we have to take it. We'll take it! Any questions?"

"No, sir," Gomez answered.

Gerhardt turned on one heel and started away. He knew we didn't like him, and we knew he didn't like us. Lieutenant Milton was called to another meeting, and he gave us a look before he went that said he was tired of meetings and getting tired of the war. But I have a good feeling about him. I think he's going to pull us through.

Some guys came over from the 1st Battalion and asked if we had any extra gas. Mink asked them if they had any extra trucks.

"We're tired of walking through these hedgerows," he said. "We're thinking of finding the main road and heading straight for Germany."

"You're the hotshot 29th, right?" The corporal speaking had a broad face and red hair that hung down from under his cap.

"We're the 29th," Gomez said. "We're supposed to be hot?"

"Jumping tall buildings with a single bound and stuff," the red-head said. "You actually see any Germans up close?"

"We try to kill them before they get too close," Gomez said. "That's because they smell bad up close. How about you guys?"

"The only time we see them is when we get the game on," the corporal answered. "The way we play is that we march along, they nail a few of us, then we chase them all over hell, then we march along, then they nail a few more of us, then we chase them, and the friggin' game goes on."

"That's about how we're seeing it, too," Mink added. "Only we're just doing it at a more leisurely pace."

We told the corporal we didn't have any trucks, let alone extra fuel, and he shook hands with a few of the guys before leaving.

"You think that everybody is doing the same thing as we are?" Gomez asked. "Because if we're all getting whacked like he said, then we're losing this war."

I hadn't thought about it before, but I knew Gomez could have been right. Maybe we were just going to be over here until all of us got killed or wounded and the Germans would win.

"What do you think, Woody?" Gomez pushed for an answer.

"I think we're making progress," I said. "We were supposed to get on shore, and we got on shore. We were supposed to move inland, and we're moving. Gerhardt says the Germans are catching hell, and I believe him. We got a pissload of prisoners on D-Day. We've captured more since then. I don't think they're getting too many of our guys."

"Yeah." Gomez looked away.

From what we could see, from what we were hearing from other units, I realized that we could be losing. It made me feel like shit.

Back home in Virginia I had always thought of France as a far-off place with young Frenchies sitting on the grass near lakes having picnics and scoffing down bottles of wine. Sometimes I would imagine myself in Paris, always in some scene from a travel poster with the Eiffel Tower over my shoulder. None of what I was seeing was that France. The whole area was more countryside than city, and the idea that behind every tree there could be a German with a machine gun changed the images in my head completely.

Lieutenant Milton came out of the meeting, and we watched as Gerhardt and some of the other brass took off. Burns went over to where Milton flopped near the base of a tree and offered him a cigarette. Milton took it and lit up. The two men talked, and then Burns turned and signaled for me and Gomez to come to him.

"What's up?" Gomez asked.

"Lieutenant?" Burns turned to Lieutenant Milton.

"Gerhardt is still talking about companies and battalions and regiments," Milton said. "Major Johns told him that none of the companies were complete, none of the battalions were up to strength, and he couldn't even recognize us as a regiment anymore."

"What did he say to that?" Gomez asked.

"He said that as long as we're companies on paper, we're companies." Lieutenant Milton's lips hardly moved as he spoke. "The way I figure is right now we have a company of fifty-three men. But we have a job to do and we need to get it done if we're going to get home again. We're pushing the Germans back, but they've got more stuff to show us. They've got panzer battalions on the way to the front to be waiting for us when we attack. We've got control of the air, so their tanks can't move in the open."

"We have tanks, too," Mink said.

I liked the idea of him saying *we*.

"We have tanks, but their panzers are bigger, better armored, and their crews are damn good," Milton said. "Until the Third Army gets its equipment into gear, their tanks are going to rule."

"So what are we supposed to be doing?" I asked. "I can't stand up to no tank."

"You can't stand up to a tank," Mink said, smiling. "*No* tank is a double negative."

"What we're supposed to do is to create and control an area in which we can bring enough equipment to overwhelm the Krauts," Milton said. "Everybody figures they know this, so they need to regroup and push us back into the sea before we get too much gear and too many men ashore for them to do it."

"And this is supposed to work?" Mink asked.

"I hope so," Lieutenant Milton said. "I really hope so. We're starting off tomorrow before daybreak, so get some rest."

Rest. Lieutenant Milton got some guys from a military police company to stand guard for the night, and we dug in and tried to sleep. I told my body to relax, but it had forgotten how. Each muscle twitched, my hands jerked in my sleep, and I woke with a start. I was frightened out of my sleep a dozen times by things I wasn't aware of. Was there a noise? Did something touch me? I didn't know. Over and over again I was suddenly awake and my heart was racing. Gomez and Mink were lying not far from me. I watched their silhouettes until I was sure they were breathing before I shut my eyes again.

■ ■ ■

Morning. The distant horizon was rimmed with light. Birds were singing, or chirping, or whatever they do just before sunrise. I peed and felt good about it. We had coffee and scrambled eggs before moving out.

Mink was behind me as we pushed down a dark road. Any moment I expected to hear the familiar burping of a German machine gun. I remembered Petrocelli saying that if you actually hear the sound of the gun then you know it missed you. It was a logical thing to say, but it didn't make walking through the muddy Normandy road any better.

We walked for an hour without receiving any fire. We were passing other companies, and sometimes stragglers. Burns didn't trust anybody. He kept telling us to watch the guys we passed, even if they were speaking English. Burns was freaking me out.

Daybreak. We were on a bluff overlooking a small cluster of houses huddled together at the end of a field. There was a stream running by the houses, and a patrol went down with water cans. We kept an eye on the houses until the men had filled the cans and were on the way back to our lines. In back of one of the houses was a smaller house, and I thought it was an outhouse. I would have liked to go see if it was, but I didn't have the nerve to go alone. I wanted to be with the guys around me. Mink was sitting at the base of a tree. Milton was sitting cross-legged, looking at some maps. Burns and Stagg were talking quietly. By himself, Gomez was checking his rifle. He was young-looking, but he looked like a soldier.

We were past the other units, and Milton called for artillery before we moved ahead. We were told that there wouldn't be any artillery unless we spotted enemy troops.

"Tell 'em you've seen some!" Stagg said.

Lieutenant Milton got back on the radio and, pinpointing an area where there might be soldiers, called for artillery again.

In a little under two minutes, our artillery opened up and we could see the explosions. Some fell short, and Stagg called in new coordinates. The barrage lasted five minutes, and then Milton had us up and moving.

"Don't bunch!"

We moved up and saw nothing. Then Petrocelli saw something and we hit the deck.

"Woody! Gomez! Check it out," Milton called.

"On the right!" Petrocelli called. "Where that branch is sticking out."

I took one side of the road and Gomez took the other. My heart was pounding, and I was gripping my rifle with both hands. As I got near, I held my hand up for Gomez to stop. I took a breath and looked closely. Two guys crouched under the branch.

"*Halten!*" I shouted at them.

They didn't move. I thought they were dead. I crept closer and saw that one of them had a huge wound in his shoulder. It was still bleeding, but he wasn't moving. Edging even closer, I saw the face of the other German soldier. One eye was open. His helmet had been hit and driven into his skull. I stood up and pulled the machine gun from between his legs.

"Search them!" Lieutenant Milton said.

I didn't want to touch them, but I made myself go through their pockets. The one with the head wound had a letter in his breast pocket, a few rounds of ammunition, and a Hershey bar.

The Enemy – Much too Close

I didn't want to be there. Not touching the dead, not trying to block out that they were as young as I was, that they had mothers and sweethearts and houses and dogs. Making sense of what they were and who they were filled me with a kind of terror, and I wanted to look away from them. Yes, and I was embarrassed. It was as if I had walked into a stranger's house by mistake and found him naked; we were both embarrassed, but he was the one who was naked and was more embarrassed than I was. But there would be nothing that he could do about how he felt, for he couldn't undo that moment when I had discovered him. It was the same with the dead. We found them lying by the side of the road, or their bodies protruded through the dense bush of the hedgerow, and they were caught in the moment, and there was nothing that they could do about it as

I fumbled through their clothing, looking for clues to who they might have been, taking souvenirs of their lives.

One day, I thought, *I might be the one lying on the road, or crumpled in the ruins of a house, or under the treads of a tank.* The dead have no knowledge of what is going on, and yet I thought, *When that moment comes, somehow I will feel the hands going through my pockets, and the great sadness of death will fall on me.*

Lieutenant Milton told us that we were just outside of Saint-André-de-l'Épine. Petrocelli pulled out his maps.

"We're the same distance from St. Lo as Roosevelt Field in Jersey City is to Yankee Stadium," he announced. "It's forty minutes by cab, and ten weeks by M1."

"Yo, Petrocelli, go tell Lieutenant Milton that we want to go to Yankee Stadium today," Sergeant Burns said.

"Summer in Yankee Stadium, that's like heaven." Petrocelli plopped down and put his legs straight out before him. "If I was in Yankee Stadium today, I'd order two hot dogs. They're trying to push sausages on people these days, but I don't trust a sausage, you know what I mean? Somehow a sausage just doesn't cut it."

"What do Germans eat?" Burns asked. "I know they eat sausages, but what else do they eat?"

"Everything," Mac answered. "The only difference between us and the Germans is that the Germans eat their big meal in the middle of the day instead of at the end of the day, the way we do."

It was two o'clock when we were told to move into Saint André. Lieutenant Milton said he needed volunteers to scout the town. Stagg went, and Gomez.

There were fields all around the town, and a small cluster of houses in the center. If it was occupied, the Germans would be waiting in the fields, dug in, all the roads zeroed in. There would be mines, too.

"Why not just call in an air strike?" Minkowitz asked.

"And if there's nobody there but the French, is it all right just to kill them?"

How do you not think that *yes* is the right answer? *Yes, it is all right to kill the French, because if we don't kill them we stand a greater chance of being killed ourselves.*

Who was answering that question? Who was living inside my body and saying that my life was more important than someone else's? How did my brain suddenly become judgmental?

We formed skirmish lines to the east of the village, breaking up into squads. The fields were covered with swaying wheat plants, but the summer wind also blew the scent of fresh herbs toward us. I remembered my grandmother Darlene planting small beds of oregano and mint in the early springtime just so she could get the occasional surprise of their scent as we went through the fields of corn and alfalfa that we grew to feed the livestock.

Mac was on the radio and he gave us the all-clear signal and pointed toward the village. I looked over at Lieutenant Milton and saw him take a deep breath, hold it, and then let it out slowly. *All clear* didn't mean a thing if the Germans were well concealed. Stagg and Gomez knew that the same as we did. All that *all clear* meant was that there wasn't a sizable amount of Krauts waiting for us. Maybe three or four with machine guns ready to kill a few of us before they were killed, and maybe they would chicken out and surrender.

We started moving forward. We had hooked up with three guys from Headquarters Company, and they were lugging heavy communications equipment. Nobody gave them a hand.

"Watch out for trip wires!"

I stopped dead in my tracks and looked down at my feet. There was a vine across the top of my combat boots. I backed off of it gently and stepped over.

The distance from the closest field was about half the distance of a football field. There was no cover. Stagg and Gomez were at the edge of the field. They had made it this far.

"You two guys! Start checking the houses!"

I looked and saw Minkowitz tightening his chin strap. I didn't know the guy who was going with him. Mink looked scared. Something told me to go with him, but nothing on me moved.

I got into a prone position and looked toward the cluster of small houses. Some of the roofs were thatched, and others were covered with a reddish material. I looked for movement, a sign of waiting Germans. Mink and the guy with him moved quickly. That was the way to go — no creeping while some guy got a bead on you. They moved quickly to the first house.

Mink flattened himself against the outside wall of the house near the front door, his rifle at the ready across his chest. He was talking! Then a young woman came to the door.

Mink lowered his rifle and talked to the girl as the other guy came up. He turned toward us and gave the thumbs-up sign.

"Could be a trick!" Mac said.

"Guess we'll find out," Lieutenant Milton said. He signaled for the rest of us to head toward the houses.

A feeling of panic gripped me. Gomez and Stagg had volunteered to go through the fields and had made it. Mink had crossed to the houses and had made it. Sooner or later it would be me on point, and I wondered if I would make it.

A few French men, mostly old, came out of the houses. There were some children and old women, too. The old women wore long dresses and aprons, and the men were in dark baggy pants.

"Check each house and put something — a canteen cup — outside the front door when the house has been cleared. Nobody relax for a minute until every house has been cleared and you're set up in a defensive position."

"We're setting up communications," the corporal from Headquarters Company said.

"You're doing what I just told you to do first!" Milton barked. "Drop your gear right there and start checking the houses."

I felt pretty relaxed as I went first into one house and then another. They both smelled of tobacco and urine. I had heard stories about Germans shooting at French people going to the outhouses.

After setting up a perimeter and guards in the fields, we took a break as Lieutenant Milton got briefed on our role in an assault on St. Lo. I remembered the last briefing: *We have to take it and the Germans have to hold it.*

"Hey, Woody, you want to trade your mashed potatoes for crackers and jam?" I looked up and saw Freihofer standing over me.

"Sure," I said, "why not?"

Crackers and jam were always good, even if the crackers were stale. Freihofer handed over the can and I handed up my mess kit and watched as he scooped out the mashed potatoes.

"Mind if I sit?"

I gestured to the ground next to me and, crossing his ankles, he collapsed into a sitting position.

"What you thinking about this war?" he asked.

"I'd sure like to be home reading about it," I said. "I don't think the people back home could combine the images. You know, how pretty all of this countryside is and then all of the killing. What do you think?"

"Stupid stuff, mostly." Freihofer stuck his fork in the mashed potatoes and pushed them to one side of his mess kit. "I'm tiptoeing along the edge of the field back there thinking about all the times I was too lazy to go to church on Sundays. You know, once I almost went all the way with a girl in the church basement. It didn't happen, but it wasn't my fault that it didn't."

"And you're thinking God is looking for some payback?"

"That stupid or what?"

"I think if I ever got in a big poker game — I don't mean even for a hundred dollars or anything like that, but a really big poker game where I was betting my life against a million dollars, that big — I'd be just like I am now. I'm scared all the time, I'm wondering what I did right in my life and what I did wrong, I'm wondering if any of it really means anything.

"The million dollars would be fine, but the only part of that bet that matters is losing your life. That's what I'm thinking over here. I don't want to be a hero, I don't want to do anything wonderful, but, oh Jesus, do I want to see home again."

"You married?"

"No."

"Got a girl?"

"Does it matter if you never went out with her but you're thinking you might have liked to if you had ever had the nerve to ask her?" I asked.

Freihofer smiled and looked away.

"How about you?" I asked. "You married? Hooked up?"

"I'm close to my dad," Freihofer said. Then he shut up.

Freihofer had changed a lot. At first he seemed pissed because we noticed he was German. Then he was just distant and avoided everybody. Now he was getting to be like the rest of us, worried about what our lives had been like, worried how people would think about us if we didn't make it back home, and maybe even how God was thinking about us.

I wrote a letter to Vernelle.

Dear Vernelle,

I guess I'm not supposed to tell you exactly where I am. Even if I do, the censors will probably black it out. Anyway, I'm thinking about you a lot and wondering if you ever think of me. There's no reason for you to think about me, except, maybe, I need somebody to have me on their mind.

Most of the things I want to say to you don't have a connection. At least there's nothing that I can say that connects with anything I've ever done or said to you. That's pretty pathetic. But I'm going to say some things anyway in this letter. Please don't let them bother you too much. Just think they are the ramblings (I like that word) of a lonely soldier.

Vernelle, I spent last winter in New York City on the Lower East Side. The apartments there are so old you wouldn't believe it. In the place I stayed, the bathtub was in the kitchen. It was covered with a slab of wood that I used as a table. I'd put my easel on the tub and draw what I saw out the window. Sometimes, on cold nights, it would be freezing in that apartment, and I would be lying there shivering and alone and wishing I had someone there with me. Now I wish that someone was you.

There's noise coming from down the road, and so I'll

"Panzers!"

The boom of the panzer guns was like the voice of doom in the night. Shells slammed against the walls of the houses and through them.

"Fall back! Fall back!" Lieutenant Milton's voice called.

Where the hell was back?

"Krauts in the field!" Burns shouted. "Gotta go in after them!"

I was running toward the fields. I saw some of our men firing from the kneeling position and started thinking we would be fighting hand to hand.

Oh, please, Jesus!

I saw the barrel of a panzer gun sticking out from one of the fields. It jerked up and the yellow-and-red flame that came out covered twenty-some feet in a second.

I fell into a prone position and started looking for targets. I couldn't see if the shadows in the fields were Germans or Americans, and I kept switching targets but I wasn't firing my weapon.

Oh, please, Jesus!

Panzers!

"Go toward the fields! Go toward the fields!"

It made no sense. The fields could have been full of Germans waiting for us. Everybody was up and moving away from the houses. The booming of the panzers went on, and I heard a loud explosion just to my left.

I wanted to get down on the ground, to dig my way into the earth, but I didn't want to be left alone.

Brrrrrrup! Brrrrrrup! The sound of a German machine gun. I had heard that sound on the beach. I had seen what those guns could do.

Grenades! One! Another one! The air was full of dense smoke.

I saw a ghost figure ahead of me.

"Halt!"

I lifted my rifle, squeezing off a shot as I did. The figure jerked backward; he was falling. I was over him, looking down into his face.

The German reached up toward my rifle. I shot him in the face. Once. Again.

The sound of a plane. I looked up. American planes were buzzing our positions. Angry hornets against the darkening skies.

The panzers started moving into the hedgerows.

I didn't want to turn back to find the man I had shot. But I did. I walked over to him and, bending over, looked into what was left of his face. There was a bullet hole just below his left eye, and another above the right.

■ ■ ■

Running. We were running in terror through the hedgerows. Above us planes swooped and dived against the panzers. There were explosions, and the very air smelled of burning.

"Regroup! Regroup and take cover!" Sergeant Burns yelled. He was on one knee and holding up an arm. His M1 was across his body.

I didn't want to stop. I wanted to keep running until the pounding in my chest stopped. But I stopped a few feet away from Sergeant Burns. My gasps were loud, and I opened my mouth wide hoping to make less noise, to make myself appear less scared, less scared than the horror I felt.

"The planes will take care of the panzers," Burns said. "Look out for Krauts trying to make it back to their lines. Keep your cover and ID your targets before shooting them."

"Burns, good work!" Lieutenant Milton was a few yards away. The left side of his face was smeared with blood. "Guys, keep your heads down and listen. Gomez, can you work your way through this hedgerow?"

Gomez made the thumbs-up sign and started squeezing through the thick branches of the hedgerow to our left.

"Woody, the same thing on the other side!"

Did he know how scared I was? Did anybody know? My legs were heavy as I moved toward the right hedgerow. It was only a few yards away, and I realized that the company was in a lane. The Germans would know about it and look to hit it with artillery soon. The embankment was steep, and in the shadows of the thick undergrowth I groped, nearly blindly, toward the top of the hedgerow.

It was only two feet wide, maybe three at the top, and I got across easily. On the other side there was a wheat field, easily two hundred yards across, and I saw there was no place to hide in it. As I huddled against the base of the hedgerow I had just climbed over, I felt relieved.

There were shots in the distance. Once in a while they grew more intense, but there were no sounds of the big panzer guns. Fighter planes circled overhead and then peeled off as they lost altitude and swooped over the fields and hedgerows.

"Woody, we're moving out," a voice said from the other side of the hedgerow.

I twisted my ankle making my way through the hedgerow again, but soon I was with my platoon. We walked four yards apart, and I could tell we were headed away from St. Lo.

"Stay alert!" Lieutenant Milton called out.

Images flashed in my mind. They were brief and jarring. The blur of wheat as we ran from the panzers. The backs of soldiers crouched and running, the roundness of their helmets forming dark silhouettes against the brown-gold wheat.

The face of the soldier I shot. I killed.

Someone was walking next to me. Stagg.

"How you doing?" he asked.

"It's getting to be work to get one foot in front of the other," I said. "That sound pretty stupid to you?"

"Were you scared back there?"

Scared? Everything inside of me wanted to scream out. I wanted to cry, to call for my mother, to close my eyes and bury my face in my hands.

"Yeah," I said. "Real scared."

"Me too," Stagg said.

I looked at him. His face was the same grim mask it had always been, the same tough-as-nails expression, the same pale white complexion that didn't seem to hold any emotions.

"I didn't expect tanks," I said.

"The fucking Germans are smart," Stagg said. "They let us into that village knowing how tired we are. Then they send in some panzers to wipe us out. We got lucky today because there were some planes in the area."

"Is that how we're going to make it through this war?" I asked. "Being lucky?"

"You got anything better?" he asked.

I didn't.

We moved slowly for another half hour, then hooked up with a small company from the 175th and a band of stragglers. The make-shift force was being led by a lieutenant colonel. He looked like the bad guy in a cowboy movie. He spoke to Milton while the rest of us sat or lay down the best we could. It wasn't so much that we were physically tired; we were emotionally tired, too.

The officers met, and when Milton came back to us, Freihofer was the one who noticed he was wearing captain's bars.

"I see you got a promotion, sir," Freihofer said. "Congratulations."

"All it means is that a lot of officers are getting killed and they need replacements," Milton said. "At the rate we're going, I'll be a general at the end of the war. But listen up: We're going to have air cover, but we're going back to Saint André.

"The Krauts are hoping that we give them a day or two before we come back," Milton went on. "That'll give them that time to bring up more armor around St. Lo."

"They think they're really going to hold it?" Burns asked.

"If they get enough armor up and concentrated, they think that we can't sustain the losses and will give it up," Milton said. "And our brass thinks we can't afford not to take the losses. Simple as that."

"It's not simple if you're the loss," Burns said.

Milton turned to Burns sharply. "Do you have a problem, soldier? Because if you do, now's the time to spit it out!"

"Yeah, I got a problem," Burns said. "God gave me a brain *and* a set of balls!"

I watched Burns turn slowly and spit on the ground as he walked away. Milton called him back twice, and then raised his M1. Then, slowly, he lowered it.

■　■　■

Burns had said what we had all been thinking, what we were saying to one another and to ourselves. The bodies were piling up faster than our minds could handle them. Gerhardt was bitching because we weren't making much progress. We seemed to be going in circles, looking for a weakness in the German lines and not finding any. None of us were confident, nobody was still thinking we had an easy win. *Don't think.* How could thinking help? In our heads we were playing and replaying our own death scenes. How could we turn off the flickering images when they came at us every day?

Don't think.

I promised myself I would do what I was told. If I was told to run across a field, screaming and yelling to shut out the sounds of my own panic, I would do it. If I was told to look into the face of some German and shoot that face away, I would do it.

Don't think.

■　■　■

"*Mister* Wedgewood!"

I turned and saw Marcus Perry grinning at me. At first I didn't think the guy in front of me was real, but when he opened his arms I knew he was.

"How you doing, man?" Marcus asked.

"Not all that good," I said. "You?"

"Better than you guys," he said. "All the reports we're hearing are about how you're kicking ass up here, but you know you're only sixteen miles from Omaha Beach. And we're carrying the bodies back."

"You hear anything from Bedford?" I asked. "You got the time to sit down?"

"Yeah," he said, with a slight nod of the head.

Marcus's face seemed leaner, less round. His build was still good, but not as heavy as it had been when he played ball back in Virginia.

"How are people taking it back home?" I asked.

"We brought mail and ammunition up," Marcus said. "So your folks should be able to tell you something. But from what I know, they got a flood of telegrams early this month saying who had been killed on the beaches. My uncle was saying that grown men were crying. They didn't expect nothing like what happened."

Early this month? We had landed at Omaha Beach on June sixth, and it was already July. It took a whole month to get those telegrams out?

"I sure as hell didn't, either," I said. "You getting any word about how the invasion is going?"

"They say the Germans are trying to get their panzers to the front," Marcus said. "They think their tanks are going to stop you guys, and they're throwing in everything they got to give themselves time to get them up here."

"What day is this?" I asked. "I mean, what day of the month?"

"The eighteenth of June," Marcus said. "You sure you okay?"

"We didn't even get to July yet?"

"Something like that," Marcus said. "You sure you okay?"

"It stopped making sense a while back," I said. "The killing just floods over you like — I don't know — like a storm you can't get out of. I don't know how I'm going to handle all of this killing when I get home. I just don't know, man."

"You think it makes more sense when one of us in these trucks gets killed? They got snipers trying to shoot the drivers and artillery trying to zero in on us. We're driving forty and fifty miles an hour with a foot and a half between trucks. I don't think I could pee straight if I was pissing down a slide rule!"

"Hey, Marcus?"

"Yeah?"

"If you get back home — what's it going to be like?"

"Beautiful like Christmas morning, Josiah," he said. "Beautiful like Christmas morning."

There was a whistle, and a black officer, blacker than any man I had ever seen, started yelling for his soldiers to mount up.

"Drive carefully!" I said.

"Hey, Josiah, God bless you!" Marcus said. "God bless you."

I knew he meant it, too.

God had never been on my mind that much, and I didn't expect him to pop up and take care of me now that I was in Normandy. But I thought about God more than I ever had. I didn't like it, but I did.

When Lieutenant Milton got promoted to captain he seemed a little friendlier, like maybe we were his boys and he had to take care of us. He got to passing out the mail personally — there weren't that many of us from the original battalion — and when he gave me a letter from my mom I was really happy. I put it in my field jacket pocket, telling myself that I would read it later, but then I took it out a minute later and, sitting against the back tire of a jeep, I read it.

Dear Son,

I hope this letter finds you well. We have heard such terrible things about the fighting. Nobody knows if their loved one is well or not. That is except for the ones who have heard that their boys were dead. It is such a sad thing. We can't sing in church or listen to the word of the Lord without thinking that we are not doing enough to keep you well. Oh how I wish this war had not happened at all.

Josiah, I love you with all my heart and I always will. I don't know what else to say. I truly don't. I feel so bad that I had not been praying for you every day until after we got the news about what happened during the invasion. We have read the newspapers and we have heard stories, but nobody can get a good picture in their minds about what it was like. Oh, please understand how much I love you and want you to come home again. Anything that I have not done in the past I will try to make up to you. We all miss you so.

When Ellen Fuller, Carter's grandmother, told us he would not be coming home again I felt so bad, I couldn't look her in the face. I feel so bad for all of the boys and wish this war had never happened. Josiah, I don't know what else to say except that I love you and I hope to hold you and see you as soon as God is willing. Please do not be concerned about our well-being or us getting on here in Virginia. It is you that we all are worried about.

Yesterday I passed by Vernelle and she held my hand and said she missed you so. That's how people feel about all of our young men, that we miss you so!

Your loving mother, Margaret DeVera Wedgewood

■ ■ ■

We marched, each with our own thoughts and our own feelings, back to the town we had been chased from. On the way there we passed two panzers that had been knocked out. Next to one there was a German soldier, black from being burned, one arm out to his right as if he was reaching for something, the other one pointing to the darkening sky. The wheat fields were burning, most of them already down to the ground level. The little group of houses that had huddled in the center of the village were now nothing more than a few jagged walls. Now and again I could see the charred remains of what might have been a person.

Waves of fatigue, each stronger than the one before, washed over me. My body was in full surrender to the war.

Wednesday or Thursday, Near the End of June, and Raining

I fell asleep standing up. When I awoke it was with a start, my rifle flying in one direction and something I had been holding in my left hand, I thought it was a book at first, against the nearby wall.

"If you can tap dance when you do that we'll take it on the road," Stagg said. "Pretty good trick."

More startled than embarrassed, I picked up my rifle, glanced at the object across the room, and remembered being offered the roll by an old man. A sort of an apology came to mind and ended in a shrug.

"What's up?" I asked.

"The captain wants you and Freihofer to question a prisoner," Stagg said. "Freihofer because he speaks German and you because you look like you got a brain in your head. You awake enough to do it?"

"I have a choice?"

"No."

"Then I'm awake enough. The guy speaks English?"

"Yeah. What they want to know from the beginning is whether or not he's a spy. They found him in civilian clothes. If he's not, they're going to want to know what outfits he was with and what their morale was," Stagg said. "And let me tell you something, Woody, they're going to want you to come up with something, so don't talk to this guy and come away with nothing. Make something up if you have to, but give them a report."

"Where is he?"

Stagg nodded toward the door and started off, and I followed. Talking to a prisoner was better than running across a field, better than shooting at Germans, and a lot better than being shot at.

Our brass was setting up in a house they had commandeered, and Major Johns was there with a general I didn't know. When Stagg stopped and saluted, all I did was to come to attention, then throw a late highball toward the general.

Freihofer was in the room, too, and there was a young man, stocky and broad-faced, standing against the wall. His right arm was in a sling, and he seemed to have trouble breathing. As Stagg had said, he was wearing civvy pants and a vest. A shirt that was too big hung outside of the pants, and I noticed that the bottom was covered with mud.

"We got a Kraut in civvies," Major Johns said. "So we have a choice of killing him outright as a spy, handing him over to the French Resistance who'll probably kill him, or taking a couple of guys out of our line to get him back to the rear. I'm in favor of shooting him, especially if he doesn't cooperate."

Johns turned and looked at the prisoner. The guy looked down at the ground, and I knew he was scared.

Johns told us to take him out to another house that Headquarters Company was setting up in and talk to him to see how much he wanted to live. I thought of what Stagg had said, and wondered if he had chosen me because there was a chance I could get out of combat by taking the guy to the rear.

Freihofer poked the guy in the back on the way to the house we were to use. There were three guys from a military police unit in the building and some clerks setting up a communications station.

The house wasn't one of the better ones I had seen. Most of the houses in Normandy were simple, with a few chairs, a table, a stove or fireplace, and rooms to sleep in. A smallish woman sat in one corner, and I imagined it must have been her house at one time.

"You speak slowly, and tell only the truth," Freihofer said to the prisoner, who sat on a box we had put in one corner. His shoulders were rounded forward, his hands clasped between his knees. "Or we'll kill you right away. You got that?"

The man nodded. He looked at Freihofer, then quickly down, then glanced at me and away again, just as quickly.

"What company were you with?" Freihofer asked after we had sat the man down.

"Grenadier Regiment 915, sir."

"You were with them for the whole war?" Freihofer asked.

"When the Amis — when you arrived and we were forced back from the beach, I was put with the 352nd, sir."

"You were on the beach? At Omaha?"

"Omaha? I don't know this word, sir," he answered slowly. "We were in front of Vierville."

"Fucking Omaha!" Freihofer's hand tightened around his M1, and I saw the German's eyes shut.

"You joined the army to kill Americans?" Freihofer sounded as if he was going to lose it.

"Not to kill anyone," the German said. "Only to save my brother."

"Where did you learn to speak English?" I asked.

"I spent a year studying in the Netherlands. We were thinking of switching our farm to raise livestock before the war."

"You said you joined the army to save your brother," I said. "How does that work?"

"We lived on a farm in Elbersberg, in Bavaria. We were not soldiers. No one in my family was a soldier —"

"According to you!" Freihofer spat the words out. I thought he was losing it.

"You want to do this by yourself?" I asked Freihofer. "If you do, just say it and I'll leave."

He looked at me hard and I returned his look. Then he gestured toward the prisoner.

"Look, they're trying to decide whether or not to kill you as a spy," I said. "So you better tell us anything you can. What did you do in — Bavaria?"

"In Elbersberg we grew hops to make beer," he said. "Sometimes we grew wheat. Small amounts of wheat. There were fourteen houses in the village. Our house was the last one in the row. One day some soldiers came and they lined up all the men and asked why we weren't in the army. They saw me and my brother Phillip and my brother Rudolf. My name is Helmut. They gave us papers to fill out and dates to report to the army. Me and Phillip were given two weeks to get our affairs in order and to report to the army for assignment. Rudolf was given the classification of *Blöde* because he is different."

"He's retarded?" Freihofer asked.

"He does not think quickly," the man Helmut answered.

"So then what happened?" Freihofer asked.

"We had heard what they were doing to men and boys who were not fit," Helmut said. "My mother began to cry, and my father wanted to take him away and hide him. But then my father said that it wouldn't do any good because they would find us and say we were deserters."

"What are you talking about?" I asked. "I'm not getting this picture."

"If a man was not — how do you say? — have all of his parts, or if he has a disease, sometimes they were taken away. It's been said they were killed," Helmut said. "They give them needles to put them to sleep and they don't wake up again."

I looked at Freihofer and he shrugged.

"So what did you do?"

"My older brother had a plan. We were, all three of us, to go and join the Grenadiers," Helmut said. "We tore up the papers the army had given us. We went south toward Nuremberg and joined an outfit that was short of its quota. Then we trained together. My brother and I looked after Rudolf and we took care of him. You don't have to be so smart to be a soldier.

"Still, it was seen that Rudolf was not too strong in his head. Some of the officers wanted to get rid of him, but they were short of men and so they used him as a worker. It's the same way that they used the ones from the East."

"You were on the beach on June sixth?"

"I was in Resistance Nest 63," Helmut said.

"What was your farm like?" I asked.

"What the hell do you want to know *that* for?" Freihofer asked me.

I didn't have a reason; I just wanted to know.

"So what happened on the beach when you saw us coming?"

Silence. After a while his lips began to move, and I could almost hear his thinking. We all knew what had happened on the beach.

More silence from Helmut.

"You going to fucking talk?" Freihofer asked.

"We didn't expect you on that day," Helmut said. "I don't know really when we expected you to come, but some of our commanders did not think you would come on the water. They thought you would all come by plane, by paratroopers. When the alarm went off and we rushed to our posts, we looked out and at first we could see nothing. Then in the distance we saw the dark outlines of the ships. We had been told we could see the smoke from the ships when they came across the channel, but there was no smoke. There were more ships than anyone had imagined.

"When the guns began it was a hard time for us. The ground shook from the explosions. We had been told that we would be safe in the nests. They were concrete over steel. Very strong. But what seemed strong to keep you out began to look . . . began to look like it was only meant to keep us in. A man in my company, he was from Metzingen, saw the boats, and we knew that you were in the boats. Somebody said it was the British, and others said it was the Amis. We couldn't tell from the nests."

"Did you work on a farm?" Freihofer asked me.

"Part-time work," I said.

"Tell him what you did on the farm," Freihofer said to Helmut.

"On the farm I got up each morning — our house had only two small windows so that it was not too cold when it snowed — and fed the animals. Then my father and my brothers and I would take the cart out to the fields to see what was there to do. When it wasn't harvest time we took care of the crop, weeding and trimming the plants. When it was harvest time, we would gather the crops and —"

"How did it feel shooting down Americans?"

"It felt like I was waiting for my death," Helmut answered quietly. "I felt that they had all come only to kill me and my brothers. At first when the boats came to the shore, and the tanks in the water, we thought we would stop you. That was the plan. But so many soldiers were falling, and still they came. Still you came. My brother said we should run. But some of the soldiers from the East, captives from the Russian front, tried to leave and they were shot down."

"By the Navy guns?" Freihofer asked.

"By our commanders," Helmut said. "After a while, the feeling came that it was all useless. I told my brothers good-bye and they told me good-bye. Rudolf thought when you shot Amis it didn't matter to them, they just got up again. There were so many. Just so many."

"What was the mood of the men?" I asked.

"I don't know this word *mood*?"

"Were they happy? *Stimmung*?" Freihofer asked. "Your soldiers, were they happy?"

"Before you came we were mostly bored," Helmut said. "Every day it was just looking out over the water and waiting. Every day listening to the radio and to our officers, who would look at the sky and at the water and make up little stories about why you would come or why you would not come. From the new people that came into our outfit —"

"The 352nd?"

"The 352nd," Helmut said. "We thought it was going badly for us. Not as bad as on the Eastern front, where the stories we heard were terrible. It was not bad sitting by the water."

"And when they saw we had come?" I asked.

"They were scared," Helmut said. "I was scared. Everybody was scared. The guns from the ships came closer and closer, and you could feel the ground shake around you. The smell was terrible. You had to know that sooner or later it would break down, that the nests would fall apart. Our officers said we would all fight to the last bullet.

"Then the Amis . . . We didn't know yet that they were Amis even though we could see their helmets. We weren't sure," Helmut said. "Some had begun to run up the hill, and we began to retreat to our first position."

"What's that mean? *First* position?"

"We had positions to retreat to before you came," Helmut said. "It seemed simple. But then we were told not to retreat. That we were to fight to the last bullet."

"How did you get into civilian clothing?"

"I was afraid," Helmut said. "I wanted to run away because I was afraid, but I was just as afraid of my commanders. They were shooting more and more people. They shot the ones from the East first, and then anybody who wanted to run away."

"Anything else you have to say?" Freihofer asked.

Helmut shrugged. "I am a shadow," he said. "There is nothing to a shadow. I am not a man anymore."

"Who cares?" Freihofer said.

"How many men from your company got off the beach?" I asked.

"I don't know."

Freihofer swung the butt of his rifle against Helmut's head.

He cried. His head down, sobbing, his hands in his lap, thinking that any moment he might be killed. He sobbed.

Freihofer asked the prisoner a few more questions, but there weren't any more answers. After a while we took him back to Major Johns and said that the morale of the regiment on the beach, the 352nd, had been bad.

"You think he's a spy?" Major Johns asked.

"I don't think so," Freihofer said.

Johns was a small man with a neatly trimmed mustache, which he kept touching. He looked at me and then at Freihofer and gave a quick nod of his head and saluted us.

The MPs took Helmut. I asked Captain Milton what I should do, and he said that Freihofer and I should go back to the company.

"You did a good job," he said.

"What's going to happen to the prisoner?" Freihofer asked.

Milton shrugged.

We heard two shots as we walked away.

The Enemy Within

Freihofer and I got back to the bivouac area, and I saw Stagg near the chow line and I headed toward him. There were three garbage cans — we called them GI cans for some reason — in a row at the end of a long table. One would have cans of food we could take, and the other two would be to wash our mess kits. Stagg looked up when he saw us coming.

"You got a problem with the way I handled that scene?" Freihofer was a half step behind me.

"You got a problem with me?" I stopped and faced him.

"Maybe I do," Freihofer said.

"What's going on?" Stagg took a step toward us.

"Woody doesn't like the way I treated the prisoner," Freihofer said. "Maybe he's getting attached to the enemy."

"Freihofer, what you were doing back there wasn't about getting information," I said. "You were trying to prove something to somebody, and I didn't give a damn about that. Hitting him in the face didn't get anything more out of him, and probably just let him know you weren't listening anyway."

"What was the German about?" Stagg asked.

Freihofer turned away and strode off.

"Not much," I said. "He said him and his two brothers joined the army at the same time. The older two guys joined so they could be with the youngest. They were afraid that the youngest guy was going to get killed by the Nazis because he was weak-minded or something. I guess you can't be a good German soldier if you're not too smart."

"Freihofer is trying to prove he's a good American soldier," Stagg said. "Guys do that. No big deal. Don't take it personally."

I tossed an *okay* to Stagg because I really liked him. Back home, in Bedford or even in New York, I wouldn't have been friends with him, but in France he was okay, even someone I admired.

There was a buzz and a lot of instant cursing. Gomez was sitting on two gas cans he had put together, and I asked him what was going on.

"All I hear is a lot of swearing," I said.

"You know I hardly ever cursed before I got into the Army?" Gomez had a nice smile. "One day I was home and I heard my mother on the phone. She was talking to my *tia* Consuela, her sister, and telling her that she had heard a lot of cursing on the bus by young men and that she was so glad I didn't use language like that. Before then I cursed some, but not that much. After that I stopped cursing altogether, until I got into the Army. I think that's all that some people understand."

"What are they cursing about?"

"We're moving toward St. Lo again tonight," Gomez said.

"Shit!"

"At 1800 hours!" Gomez said. "I'm sure the Germans know exactly when we're coming, how many infantry will be on the line, how many machine guns. They know everything about us and then get us in their sights as we come dancing up to wherever they are. We're like those clay pigeons they have at Coney Island. You ever been to Coney Island?"

"Yeah, once," I said. "Once."

St. Lo seemed to be some kind of curse we all had to face. From the first day we had struggled across the beach we were told that our eventual objective would be a dot on a map called St. Lo. They kept giving us estimates on when we would reach it and sending men across the fields and across the hedgerows to get there. And all we did was go back and forth and leave dead men for markers along the way.

I remembered what Mink had said, about how many feet we would make for each death, and tried again to push his words out of my consciousness.

I wanted to think about Coney Island. Not about the march toward St. Lo, not about the Germans waiting for us, or Freihofer, or the prisoner we questioned. I wanted my mind to be a thousand miles away. And I knew it wouldn't be, probably that it would never be.

I went to Coney Island with a girl I met in art school, Tina Aumack. She was a flirt, with a wide smile, a potty mouth, and a big chest that she liked to rub on any man who got near her. We had tried the bumper cars for an hour and then switched to the merry-go-round, with Tina sitting on my lap. She was hoping to get me excited, I guess.

She had.

I had an hour to go before we were to start out, and I decided to write a letter.

Dear Vernelle,

Things are going well here. We are advancing steadily, but slowly. There is no reason to rush as long as we get the job done, and everybody more or less agrees to that. How are things at home? Sometimes I find myself thinking about home and I can't seem to remember as much as I want to, even about places I knew very well. I hope the people in town are not fearful for us. It must have been a shock to get news of our landing. We have calmed down since then and are hoping for the best.

Every day I am hoping to hear the news that the Germans have surrendered. It would be a wise thing for them to do, but from my point of view people don't often do wise things in war.

Again, I am hoping that my writing to you does not put a burden on you. Supporting the home front must be difficult enough as it is. Most of what I know about the war is from the newspapers even though I am in the middle of the whole thing. What I see is that our guys have entered Cherbourg, which is a really big deal because it is the biggest seaport around and the Krauts really wanted to hang on to it. It seems that when we find out what they want we make sure to take it from them.

I am trying to think of what I will do after the war. Do you know what you want to do? Are you going to stay in Bedford? There is so much about you that I would like to know.

Yours truly, Josiah Wedgewood

I already knew that I wouldn't send the letter. There was nothing in it about what I really wanted to say. If it was in there, I would be saying that I need somebody to care for, and maybe somebody who would be waiting for me when I got home. I hadn't said any of that. What I thought, maybe what I knew, was that I was going to have to learn to be a civilian one day.

■ ■ ■

We were moving out. It was still light out and would be until a little after nine.

There was a steady stream of our bombers passing us overhead. I was glad the Germans didn't have much of an air force left. Their artillery was bad enough. A thought popped into my head, and I tried to ignore it. I checked my ammo, taking out the clips and tapping them against the stock of my rifle as I walked, the way I had seen Stagg do once. My legs were tired, but they would run if they had to, or jump or leap into whatever safety my eyes saw, or thought they saw. My reactions weren't thought out anymore, they just happened. That was good, I thought. For now. But would I always have the right reaction? What if I needed to think? Could I do it?

Push it away. Think about Helmut working on his farm in Bavaria. Remember the pictures of Bavaria that you've seen over the years. Hills in the background, azure skies, sunlight gleaming white against the snow-crested hills, the intense green of the crops. What color would hops be this time of year? Pale green with low plants that don't yet need support for the fall harvesting.

I forced myself to think of Helmut working with his two brothers. If they were like Americans on a small hops farm, then their mother worked along with the men part of the time and kept the house. What did she think when the Nazis talked about taking the boy? What did she think when all of her sons went off to war?

We were making our way through a small wood because the Germans had the roads zeroed in. Every once in a while a shell hit close by, and we knew that it was meant to keep us guessing. If we walked the roads they would hit us, and then they would send random shells for the areas between the roads. Headquarters Company had sent around a memo that the German artillery was being directed from St. Lo. I didn't believe it. I thought the Germans were a bunch of superhuman freaks who knew our every movement and a hundred ways of killing us.

As I walked I imagined German plots to trap us, and I was sure that I was completely right. We walked through the forest and it was growing dark. When Milton stopped us, I thought we must've been within two miles, perhaps less, of the village.

"Take ten!" Milton called out. "Keep the butts covered. Remember the three-man rule!"

If a Kraut sees a man light up a cigarette, he picks up his rifle. He zeroes in toward the light as the second man lights up. The third man is killed.

Freihofer sat next to me. I wanted him to move, but I didn't want to say it.

"I don't want to look at these people as human beings, Wedgewood." Freihofer ran delicate fingers across his forehead. "I just want to see them as the enemy. That's it. I don't mean to give you a hard time, but I'm looking at the best way to be to get myself home in one piece. You get my drift?"

"Yeah, I do," I answered. "No hard feelings, man."

"Good," he said, extending his hand.

We shook hands, and it looked as if he had started to relax a little.

"You worried about St. Lo?" I asked him. Stupid remark, just something to say.

"You know what I don't understand?" Freihofer asked.

"What?"

"Lindell is the center for the Yankees, right? Probably the best center fielder they'll ever have," Freihofer said. "But they win more games when he doesn't hit than when he does. They played the Cleveland Indians the other day. Their whole team — the Indians — is crap except for the shortstop, some clown named Lou Boudreau. You tell me how a shortstop is not 1-A and headed for the infantry — but their whole team is crap and the Yankees beat them 4–0 on the sixth. Lindell doesn't get one hit and they win. And he's the cleanup hitter! How do you figure that?"

"Who knows?" I said. The question had come out of nowhere, and I didn't have an answer. I remembered Stagg saying that Freihofer was trying to prove something. What the hell did Lindell, standing in a patch of green out in center field of Yankee Stadium, have to do with anything?

I thought, *What is Freihofer pushing out of his mind?*

As we rested I could hear our artillery in the background. The air was growing heavy and little wisps of smoke settled among the trees as the sun set.

I didn't want to talk to Freihofer anymore. I didn't want to hear his reasons for acting stupidly, or for hitting the prisoner.

I didn't want to think about Helmut, either, but the thoughts kept pushing through my head. It was like a headache I was trying to ignore. It was there and it wasn't going to go away. *Had they killed Helmut? Had they always planned to kill him?*

I remembered sitting in infantry basic listening to a droning lecture on the Uniform Code of Military Justice. The lecturer, a major, kept up a monotone for over an hour about how serious the Army was about discipline and following the rules of the Geneva Convention.

Freihofer was coping, trying to get by. Helmut had been coping, but he had had the misfortune of being captured. First, in a way, by the Germans. Then by us.

I thought of the farm he had lived on, and of his brothers. What did they look like? In my mind I brought up a pleasant scene, the kind none of the kids I had met at Cooper Union had seen because New York kids were too sophisticated. In the scene there was a broad sky interrupted by majestic Bavarian hills. Maybe there would be some livestock in the foreground. It would be a bright, sunny scene with little contrast and less meaning unless you found truth in the optimism of simple people doing simple things.

At 2145, less than an hour after sunset, all hell broke loose. The woods behind us lit up with gunfire.

Shooting in the daylight is scary. Some guys aim carefully, picking their targets; others just shoot in the general direction of the enemy. Shooting at night is insane. You can't see your target; all you see is an occasional silhouette and the sudden light from a muzzle flash. If you see the flash and you're not hit, you might survive. If someone sees your muzzle flash they have to shoot at it. In the dark, we are all enemies.

"Everybody down!" Captain Milton called out. "Keep your ears open."

I was on my knees. Alone in the dark and terrified, listening to the sound of my own heartbeat. The quick *pop-pop-pop* of rifles and the burping noises of the machine guns slowed to an occasional flurry. The night was a beast coughing in the darkness. Nobody knew who was shooting unless *they* were shooting, and nobody knew who they were shooting at — only the dying knew for sure.

We waited for minutes. Then there was a rustle near me. Frozen, I gripped the stock of my M1 as tightly as I could. The rustle stopped. Was it a breeze?

Voices. American by the cursing. Milton was up and telling us to move forward. I heard him on the radio, trying to find out what the shooting was about.

"A cow got loose," he said. "It came crashing through the hedgerow."

"They kill it?" Gomez's voice seemed higher now that I couldn't see him.

"Yeah," Captain Milton said. "I guess they did."

July 14 — Some Kind of French Holiday

"Hey, Headquarters Company is looking for an artist! Anybody here know how to draw?" A thin, redheaded corporal stood facing us on the chow line.

"Look how clean this guy is," Petrocelli said. "We wouldn't even let him into Hoboken looking like that."

"What's up?" Captain Milton asked.

"General Gerhardt wants somebody who can draw a map," the corporal said.

"Woody, you want to give it a try?" Milton asked. "You went to art school, right? I'll make sure they save you some food."

"Draw a path out of here," Gomez added. "Just in case they forgot where home is."

"Hey, Woody, I knew a guy who worked for Keuffel and Esser on Hudson Street in Hoboken," Petrocelli said. "He was in World

War I, and they took him out of the trenches to be an artist. This could be your ticket home."

I followed the corporal over to Headquarters Company. He was clean, as Petrocelli said. And a little stupid. He asked me if I didn't think the guys could have cleaned up a little.

"We're waiting for our other suits to come back from the cleaners," I said. Then said it again in my head but with a few curse words in it.

In the tent I saw Major Johns along with General Gerhardt. Johns asked me if I was a real artist.

"I guess," I said.

"If you're not the real McCoy, you'd better go back to your outfit," he said, smiling.

Gerhardt came over and looked me up and down like he was inspecting me. As far as I was concerned, he was a hard-ass and I didn't like him.

"I need to show the men what they've been fighting for and where they're going," he said finally. "I have a small map that contains every small town and village in Normandy. What I need is to blow it up with only the towns I tell you to put in it. You follow that?"

"Yeah."

"Yeah?"

"Yes, sir!"

It was an easy job. Gerhardt had a large sheet of white paper I would use to draw on, and all I had to do was put a grid on it to get the proportions right. I took the map to a table they had cleared off for me and sat down. Gerhardt sat next to me and started explaining what I would be doing. He smelled like tobacco.

"This is the Cotentin Peninsula," he said. "The Krauts have bottled us up here since we landed. All of our supplies are coming in through Cherbourg, and that's not easy. But the main thing is that we're fighting through this damned hedgerow country, which is nothing but defensive terrain. We need to break out into the open country and then we'll see what the Germans can do. And they'll see what we can do.

"We take St. Lo, cut off this peninsula, and we're on our way to the Seine. I need to explain this to the men in clear and certain terms. You need to draw me the map I need to pull it off. Got it?"

"Got it, sir."

What Gerhardt was saying made sense, but I was shocked to see how close we still were to the beaches we had landed on. The distance from Omaha to where we were was less than the distance between Bedford and Roanoke. My father had driven us down to Roanoke in less than an hour to go shopping.

The map was easy to do, but I took my time and made sure that it was as accurate as possible. Gerhardt watched me closely, sometimes grunting his approval. When I finished he offered me a cigar, which I took even though I didn't smoke.

Back with the company, I told the guys what I had done.

"How's it looking?" Gomez asked. "They sound confident up there?"

"They're not the ones taking the ground," Captain Milton said before I could answer. "We're the ants crawling over these damned maps."

It was a good image: a bunch of tiny ants crawling over a map of Normandy.

■ ■ ■

It was raining when Mink and I went on patrol. We had to go eighty yards out and along the hedgerow to see if the Germans were trying to sneak up on us during the night. Usually they didn't come at night, but once in a while they did just to keep us loose.

"Woody, you think you could be an officer?" Mink asked.

"We'll all be officers by the time this thing is over," I said. "How many guys do you think will have to die before we take out the Germans?"

"Before we reach the Seine?"

"Gerhardt thinks it's going to be easy," I said.

" 'The red fool-fury of the Seine, Should pile her barricades with dead,' " Mink said.

"What the hell did you say that for?" I asked.

"Tennyson, poet laureate of England, wrote it," Mink said. "It's about a friend of his who died at twenty-two. Kind of a bitter poem, and strange. He was probably drunk when he wrote it."

"He drank a lot?"

"I don't know." Mink's face broke out into a wide grin. "But since he's not here to defend himself . . ."

I liked Mink a lot. It was nice imagining his head being full of poetry and literature that he could call up at any moment. The thought came to me that the difference between people was not so much what they did but what they carried around in their heads. Whenever Mink opened his mouth something interesting came out, and I could imagine him getting old and people gathering around him just to hear what he had to say.

What was going around in my head wasn't much. It wasn't that I didn't have anything inside; it was just that I was tired of thinking when what we had to keep our minds on was staying alive.

We walked the patrol, up one side of the hedgerow and down the other. One time I thought I heard something.

"What is it?" Mink asked.

"Do you hear anything?"

What it sounded like was somebody snoring. It could have been an animal, or it could have been a German who had fallen asleep on *his* patrol. Or maybe even an American from a different outfit who was sleeping out in the fields. Either way, if it was a soldier and we scared him, there would probably be some shooting, and someone getting killed.

Mink tapped me on the shoulder and made some motions with his fingers that we should get the hell out of there. We did.

■ ■ ■

0500. An officers' briefing. Everyone down to major was called in, and Gerhardt explained our mission to them. Then they explained them to us. They had seen my map and ran it down just the way Gerhardt had explained it to me.

"Patton's going to be in this one!" a colonel said. "He's got his tanks down from Cherbourg and they're ready. The Brits and Canadians are getting ready for a big show near Caumont. That's where the Germans are concentrating their defense. They'll take on the Krauts there and tie them up while Patton swings around them. It's going to be great!"

We were to push off toward St. Lo again at 0800.

Everybody Is Fighting This War

We had chow, and then about ten Canadians came into camp. They were full of piss and vinegar and wisecracks.

"We heard you boys needed some help over here," one of them, a big broad-faced guy with a ruddy face, said. "And since a soldier's duty is to fight and take care of the local ladies, we thought we'd let you fight, and we'll take care of the lady problem. Keep your heads clear for the job ahead."

"Did you bring any food with you?" Petrocelli asked.

"Naw, we order out!" said a skinny soldier with a faded uniform who was squatting near the small fire we had built. "We thought you Americans were catering!"

"Tell them about the Yank food truck we found," a small Canadian with bad teeth said.

"We were coming down from Cherbourg, through the bloody hedgerows, and catching it pretty hard," the skinny one said. "There was a lull in the fighting, and we were about ready to call it a night when we heard a truck coming down the road as big as you please. We looked and it was a Yank truck, so we relaxed.

"Only it was a Yank truck that the Germans had captured. The guy driving the truck was so happy with himself that he took a wrong turn and drove right up to us. There were two Jerries in the back, and they were back there going through your food like it was Christmas in Berlin. We captured them and your truck. Now the big deal is whether we should take them back to Britain or send them out to get another Yank truck because — to tell you the truth — the food wasn't half bad!"

"If you guys like what they're serving us," Petrocelli said, "then you gotta be desperate!"

"How come you're over here with us now?" Captain Milton said.

"To pick up supplies," the Canadian said, his voice suddenly softer. "Burial stuff."

That ended the conversation.

Ten minutes before we were to shove off toward St. Lo, we got hit with an artillery and mortar barrage. In the damp morning, the smell of cordite mixed with the sickly sweet smell of dead animals to form a heavy curtain of pure and nauseating stink. Shells hitting the trees seemed to explode into firework displays, and the shells that missed the trees sent columns of dark earth into the air. There was no place to run. If they missed you then you lived, and if they didn't you were dead.

Our guys got on the radio to call for an answering barrage. Half the telephone lines were cut, and nobody was sure how many of the messages were getting through to our artillery. Overhead, cub planes tried to spot their gun positions.

My body shook with the earth and trembled in between the blasts. No one spoke. It was almost as if we didn't want to call attention to ourselves, as if we were trying not to let the shells, or the Germans, or God, know where we were.

I prayed. Not for God to save my life, because I didn't think he was listening to us anymore, but because the pounding and the noise had gotten into me and had pushed everything out except a few prayers, a smattering of curses, and an urge to pee.

The medics moved from hole to hole, giving whatever comfort they could to the wounded. I noticed that none of the wounded screamed out for help. They would just lift a bloody arm, or thrash about silently until someone noticed them.

The pounding went on for a full ten minutes before it stopped.

"We got movement!" This from a radio man.

Movement. German soldiers moving toward our position. We dug in, checked our rifles, looked for something to hide behind, and waited. Seconds later, there was shooting.

"They're trying to knock out the cub!" Petrocelli called out.

The cub plane, small and fragile in the thick air, looked like an awkward dragonfly against the gray sky. It dropped a flare over the Kraut troops coming in.

I saw the plane lurch and spin as one wing was ripped by a burst from a machine gun. The plane twisted, rose, and then leveled off as it headed away.

Then more planes, thankfully ours. P-38s peeling off and shooting at the enemy, dropping bombs that looked like a row of sticks falling to the ground. More explosions. Nothing to think about except to wait for the sight of the Nazi helmets.

Two men moved up with a bazooka from the chow area and started making their way toward a low brick fence that faced what once had been a small feed barn. Two fighter planes, one coming very low, the other up and behind him. A burst of gunfire, and the two men went down.

"Wave them off! Wave them off! They hit our guys! They hit our guys!"

Several of us stood and waved frantically at the planes. They circled, then took off.

And then the attack was over. It had been beaten off. A chaplain got to the men with the bazooka before I did. I saw the bodies, one lying facedown and the other crumpled on his side. They were both dead. The man on his side was Freihofer.

A panzer had been hit, and several Kraut soldiers lay dead on the roadside. There were two wounded Germans, their bodies

shaking from the pain, and now from the cold rain that had begun
to fall.

■ ▦ ▩

"I finally figured what 'being in reserve' means," Stagg said. "It's
when the incoming artillery, mortars, and sniper fire don't start until
after we have our chipped beef on toast in the mornings."

"It beats the hell out of running across a field toward a hedgerow,"
I said.

"I'm getting faster." Burns was puffing on a cigar he had bummed
from a Frenchman. "Either that or me closing my eyes when I'm running makes it seem faster."

I wasn't getting any faster. The thought had come to me to run
as fast as I could, but then I thought that if I was out front the
Germans would think I was special and pick me off first. But then
if I ran in the pack they might try to shoot into the pack to be sure
to hit somebody. Thinking had slowed me down all my life, and now,
when I needed it most, it still wasn't helping.

One good thing about being in reserve was that the supply
trucks could almost always make it and the mail and food reached
us three times a week. We got extra ammunition, toilet paper,
and first aid kits the first day. The bad part was that guys were
still getting killed. The Krauts couldn't move their tanks by day
because we were controlling the skies and a plane with a bomb could
wipe out the biggest tank. But they could still send over artillery, as

Stagg said, and there were little pockets of German squads all over the area.

I got three letters at mail call. One was from my mother, and two were from Vernelle. My hands were shaking when I read Mom's letter.

Woody, Baby,

Please take care of yourself. By that I mean for you to be kind of selfish and look out for your own needs. I know you are not that kind of young man, but please do it for me, as I am so nervous about your being over there. I remember you did very well in French at Moneta High, and I hope it is coming in useful. The newspapers say that you are chasing the Germans all over France. Do not get too close to them, especially if they have guns. I guess they would all have guns, but you know what I mean.

Things are going well here, so there is no need for you to worry about anything. When you come home I would love to spend some time with you before you go back to school in New York City. Of course I will keep your room ready if you decide to stay a while. Ezra is keeping it neat (for Ezra). Vernelle Ring said to tell you hello. I didn't know you knew her that well, but she seems like a very nice girl.

Uncle Joe has a cough, but it is nothing to worry about. He is taking rum and honey for it, and I think he rather enjoys having it.

Everyone in the church has you and all the boys in their prayers. The Gold Star Mothers sit together and keep their heads high even though their hearts are heavy.

Woody, don't think of taking care of yourself as not caring about your fellow man. I know you care about everyone.

Aunt Anna, Marcus's mother, said that he saw you in England and that you were looking well. I asked her if they had a Gold Star Club in her church, and she said that they did not.

Please write when you can, but if you can't I'll understand.

Your loving mother, Margaret

Of the two letters from Vernelle, I read the second letter first, figuring she had had time to think about us more.

Dear Josiah,

Please, please disregard my last letter. I am so ashamed of myself for saying what I did and for mailing the letter off so quickly. I went down to the post office the next day, but it was already gone. I feel so stupid. If you can forgive me, I would like to write to you again, and in the future I promise to be more intelligent in what I write.

I spoke to your mother yesterday. She has worried herself sick about you and the other boys from town. We pray for each of you every day. But that doesn't seem to stop the flow of telegrams that keep coming from the government. I hope this letter finds you well and I hope that you can forgive my first letter as the crazy ramblings of a nineteen-year-old girl who thought she was being clever.

Yours, Vernelle Ring

I didn't want to read the first letter right away, hoping to keep it for a later time. I really wanted the second letter to say something about her liking me, but it hadn't. Her wanting to write to me didn't mean much, or at least I didn't think it meant much.

Our battalion, or what was left of it, was moved another mile back, and the rumor was that we were going home. Then Captain Milton said that the docks at Cherbourg and off the beaches had been damaged and we were low on supplies again.

"So since you didn't have any bullets to shoot at the Germans, Uncle Charlie decided to give you a vacation," he said. "And they're sending a lot of material to the Canadians."

"Why?" Gomez asked. "They don't know that friggin' Canada is another friggin' country?"

"They know that, Gomez," Milton said. "But they're going to ask the Canadians and the British to attack the Germans' strongest position, where they have the most tanks and the most men. They're going to attack head-on so that the Krauts can't call in any reserves to defend St. Lo. If it works, we'll look great. If it doesn't, we'll suffer. Either way, the Canadians are going to lose a pissload of people."

"Shit," said Gomez.

"My thought exactly," Milton said.

"Is that whole plan still going to happen?" I asked. "We're going to capture St. Lo in sixteen minutes, then run over and stop the Germans from attacking the flanks while Patton does an end around for the touchdown?"

"And if it works on paper, it's got to work in real life," Captain Milton said.

A USO troupe came and set up loudspeakers and passed out coffee, chocolate bars, and donuts. Guys who didn't even drink coffee were lining up just to see some Americans who smelled a little like civilians. There were seven people traveling with the USO van, and four of them were women. They had three drivers and some MP guards. I watched for a while as they were setting up, then opened the other letter from Vernelle.

Dear Josiah,

It was such a thrill to hear from you. I am so glad that you have not been killed or wounded. Josiah, from the first day that I heard you were going off to study art in New York City, I was thinking of going to New York to follow you. I didn't know what I would do in a city that big, but just the thought of it, the two of us away from our little town roots and fancy-free, got my head spinning!! I thought we could live together in a walk-up apartment the way artists do in motion pictures. I even thought up some background music! Can you imagine that?

And about the living together business — I didn't think we had to do it as man and wife; I just pictured us in the apartment, with you painting pictures and me maybe going to school at night and working in the daytime.

I don't know what I want to do with my life, but I do know that I do not want to spend my life with a man who is dumb or who is not wanting to have a more exciting life than the guys here in Bedford. What I wanted, I think, was to be swept off my feet, and your letter did exactly that.

Josiah, I do not know you that well, but I think I have a good idea of the man you are and I LOVE THAT MAN.

I was listening to some songs on the radio, and the one I like best is "I'll Walk Alone" by Dinah Shore. I've been a little lonely, and thinking about you being lonely at the same time, even though you are so far away, is a great comfort to me.

Josiah, I cannot wait to mail you this letter. I am already seeing you reading it somewhere in France with your uniform on and your rifle leaning against a tree. That is so romantic to me, but I imagine to you that is old hat by now. I look forward to seeing you again and this time really getting to know each other.

'Til Then — Vernelle

I wasn't supposed to be thrilled or anything even coming close to it, but I was. Girls had never made a lot of sense to me before. My body reacted to them, my mind sort of chased them around, but I had never been serious about a girl. Now I was falling-down serious about Vernelle Ring, a girl I could only half remember from my days in Bedford, and who I wanted as much as anything I had ever wanted. They always say there are no atheists in a foxhole. Maybe, but I know there is no one in a foxhole who doesn't want someone to love.

July 16

The five days out of the fighting were good, but thinking about starting in again was the worst thing. Freihofer had said it best: If any of us had known what we were going to be facing on the beach that day, what we would see and how many of us would be dead, they would have had to shoot us on the *Thomas Jefferson* to get us off of it.

Gerhardt came by again and smirked about killing Germans. He said that General Patton was so eager to get into the war, he could "taste it."

We captured more Germans. Some of them were only boys. Even the older ones were younger than the ones we had faced on the beach.

"'Men who went out to battle, grim and glad.'" Mink's soft, high-pitched voice seemed to come out of the air, not from his skinny, unshaven head. "'Children, with eyes that hate you, broken and mad.'"

As much as I liked Mink, I was also starting not to like him. He gave words to everything. Words that he was pulling out of a memory crammed with too damned much to reason with and words you didn't want bouncing around your own skull.

The Germans were surrendering faster and faster, and yet our officers were picking up the same messages from Berlin: They were being told to fight to the last bullet.

Captain Milton asked me to question two of the new prisoners. I told him that I didn't speak German, but he shrugged me off. I was to talk to the prisoners with Petrocelli. I knew Petrocelli wanted to shoot them. I think that's what they would have done to them in Hoboken.

The prisoners were a young man and an old guy. The old man was a hundred years old, maybe a thousand. His neck was wrinkled and gray, and his hands were shaking. His lower lip was larger than his upper, which made him look a little like a baby. Neither of the prisoners spoke English, or at least that's what they suggested with their gestures. Petrocelli searched the old man and found a card in his pocket with a picture of Jesus on it. He put it in his own pocket.

Then Petrocelli started searching the young soldier. The tall, wide-shouldered grenadier looked at Petrocelli with clear contempt, and Petrocelli spat in his face. Then the contempt turned to fear as the soldier realized that he was only a trigger-squeeze away from being dead.

I opened his jacket and found a small, rectangular book in his inside pocket. It looked vaguely official, and I took it. We put the prisoners on the ground, back to back, and waited for Milton to come back.

Some of the guys came over and took turns looking at the prisoners. Some put the muzzles of their rifles against their heads just to scare them. I didn't think it was right, but I didn't say anything. I knew all the guys were sick of this war, sick of all the killing, and wanted to find a way of getting their frustrations out.

Milton came back and we turned the prisoners over to him, along with the book. He looked at it and shook his head, then started leafing through it quickly.

"Look at this!" he said. "This is a Command list of the 29th. And in the 116th, 2nd Battalion, they've got Charles N. Cawthon listed. His name is Charles R. Cawthon. How do you think they made a mistake like that?"

Captain Milton let us look at the book again before taking it and the prisoners to Headquarters Company.

"You believe that crap?" Petrocelli's eyes widened as he looked at me. "They know everything about us!"

"You see what they had about you?" I asked.

"They had . . . You're kidding me. Woody, I'm going to get you back in Hoboken and mash your head in with a pool cue!"

■ ■ ■

We were on the move again, and I wondered if anyone really knew what they were doing. The Germans still controlled the high ground, and their artillery and mortars were chewing us up. A Colonel Reed — I'd never seen him before — waved us off the road.

"Yeah, stay off the roads because the Krauts have them zeroed in." Petrocelli had his steel pot on the back of his head. "Didn't anyone tell these clowns you can't get equipment through the friggin' woods?"

Petrocelli was right. The woods were too dense for trucks or anti-tank weapons.

"I blame the French for all of this," Mink said. "Look at the way they've got their country laid out. The hedgerows are like killing grounds. The roads are just places to get blown away, and you can't see far enough to even get a good look at the enemy. What kind of layout is that to fight a war in?"

"He's right," Petrocelli chimed in. "Maybe we ought to start blasting a few Frenchies. I bet if you shot one he'd say 'Gott im Himmel!' or something like that."

Mink looked at me and shrugged. I knew he was wondering if Petrocelli was kidding or not. It didn't make a lot of difference. We were coming together. If Mink and Petrocelli could hold a conversation that made even a little sense, it meant we were really getting into one another.

Colonel Reed called up three bulldozers from somewhere and got them started clearing a path through the woods. It looked like a bad idea.

"The Germans spot that and they'll send enough 88s our way to make it look like the Fourth of July," Stagg said.

The first bulldozer got thirty yards before getting knocked out. The driver was killed and his body was hanging from the side of the vehicle. Two guys pulled him out and away from the wrecked vehicle. The rest of us stopped moving and dug in. I got the feeling we'd be stuck for a while.

I read Vernelle's letter again. She was right, it was rash and romantic and even a little schoolgirl silly, but I loved it. I *wanted* to think of her back home waiting for me and thinking about me. I thought of writing a letter to her saying how much I loved her. It wouldn't have been true — I hardly knew the girl — but I just wanted to say it.

It had been almost six weeks since we landed on the beach. It seemed like six years. The rain had come down hard the last three days, and we were all cold and soaked through.

It rained hard in the morning and harder in the afternoon. Not just plain rain, but the kind that goes right through the skin and into your bones and gets so cold, your whole body shakes. I hated the rain, and there was nowhere to go to get out of it. We wrapped our canvas half shelters around our shoulders. Mine had a rip in it just to add to my misery.

"But you gotta remember," Burns said as he checked on his squad, "there's a Kraut out there somewhere getting just as wet and just as cold as you are. With any luck he's got hemorrhoids, too. And he knows he's losing this damned war. Now don't it make you feel good knowing that?"

Stupid, but it did make me feel a little better.

The Germans didn't send across their afternoon wake-up call, and I fell asleep for nearly an hour. That was when Mink shook me and told me we were moving out again.

No trucks, no jeeps, no heavy equipment. Just a bunch of dog-tired soldiers in two columns snaking our way through the Normandy forest. Captain Milton put Gomez on point and gave us the order to move out. I could see the look on his face that said the idea sucked.

"We've spread out three battalions, all moving toward the ridges that overlook St. Lo," Milton said. "Our orders are to take the ridges, and then take the town. Our company . . . or our guys . . . are going to take the east ridge overlooking St. Lo. We'll be about a thousand, five hundred meters away."

"Yo, and let me ask you this, Captain." Petrocelli held one finger up as if he were going to say something profound. "Have we called ahead to let the Germans know we're on our way? I hate just to drop in on them with no warning."

Captain Milton started to say something, but then he just cracked up. It was one of those things that was funny and not funny at the same time. It was funny because it was so formal, as if we were going over to the Krauts' house for dinner, and not funny because they knew we were coming and would be waiting to kill as many of us as they could.

We sloshed through the rain and the mud and the cold like silent gray ghosts, lost souls shuffling in a hellish purgatory. I thought of Mom. She would have told me to change my socks because the ones I was wearing were soaked.

We were told not to talk because we didn't want the Germans to hear us, in the likely case they had outposts in the woods, and attack. Petrocelli asked how damned close the Germans were, and Milton shrugged. I wondered if we were going to make it back from this march. The Germans didn't like to fight at night, and it was growing dark. That was good. But the only time they could move their tanks and antitank guns was at night because of our planes, so we didn't know what we were going to run into.

We had walked for nearly two hours before Gomez slipped back and gave us the signal.

"Get down! Get down!" A frantic whisper from Milton.

We were bunched, and I saw Burns signaling for us to spread out. There were a little over forty men left in our company, and we were divided up into six squads of seven men each. We got down into the grass and waited for the signal to move again. I put my head to the ground, knowing that if any tanks were moving nearby I would hear their rumble. If the Kraut that Burns was talking about, the one just as cold and wet as me, was anywhere near, I hoped he was as miserable, too.

The rain against my helmet sounded loud enough for every German in Normandy to hear, but I knew it was just because I was wearing the damned thing. The thing about hiding in the forest and waiting is that you always wonder if you've missed something, if the Germans have spotted you and are sneaking up on you, or if your guys have left and you're all alone. We listened, and I prayed.

God, please get me out of this shit!

The rain let up slowly. I was sweating and stinking so bad, I thought the Germans could smell me. Then we began to hear noises, and worse. What we heard were German voices. They sounded like casual conversations, and I realized that we had wandered into a Kraut camp. Suddenly, being scared had a place and a time. There was movement around me, and I stuck my head up and watched as Stagg, Gomez, and Captain Milton huddled together. Then Gomez, somehow making his small body even smaller, came over to me.

"Woody, we got to head back and see if we can find a way out of this!" Gomez said.

This is it! the little voice in my head kept saying. *You're going to be killed today. This is it!*

I was following Gomez as we crouched as low as we could, heading along the same road we had come along. I couldn't see a damned thing and more sensed where Gomez was than anything.

Somewhere to my left I heard an engine start up. Maybe it was off to my right. We edged closer to where the sound was coming from and saw two German soldiers in short sleeves. They were drinking from what had to be their mess gear.

The machine the Krauts had started looked like a generator of some kind. What I knew was that they didn't know a bunch of Americans had drifted into their lines. Gomez and I crawled back toward our guys. We found Milton and he looked the way I felt, scared out of his mind and ready to give up.

"We can't stay here until they find us," he said. "I don't think they have the manpower to hold prisoners. We're cut off from the back and one side for sure, maybe both sides. We don't have a choice. We move forward and hope God don't *sprechen die Deutsch.*"

I had never tasted fear before, but now it was in my mouth and filling my nose with its stench. The sounds of Germans talking were all around us.

A dog barked.

Someone was pounding metal against metal.

The heavy scratching sound of someone digging came in a slow, steady rhythm.

Minutes passed. Minutes of crawling through the darkness until the sounds of the Kraut camp were behind us. I was sweating. I had to pee.

When we got to a spot we thought was clear, Captain Milton told us to take five. He found a map from somewhere and called in our position. Command Post didn't believe us.

"We're lost in the woods and they don't believe us," I said to Mink.

"Lost?" The right side of Mink's face was lit up in the sun while the rest of it was in shadow. A ghostly abstraction. "Physically or metaphysically?"

"Mink, stop thinking," I said. "You're losing me."

"Yeah, okay."

We kept moving up, inching our way through the woods, until we reached a small clearing. On the far side of the clearing, no more than a hundred yards away, there was a half-track with a gun mounted. It could have been an 88, but more likely a field artillery piece. It was partially covered by netting and tree branches to keep it from being spotted by our planes.

"We can work around the edge of the clearing, along the tree line, and take that damned thing out," Stagg said.

"Too risky," Milton said. "We'd get blown away before we got close."

"How many men will that thing take out?" Stagg asked.

"Who knows?" Milton answered. "Look, there's a time to be a hero and . . ."

Stagg had already moved off into the darkness. It was a time to be a hero. A drop of ice-cold sweat ran down the inside of my leg.

"If there's an exchange of fire, we'll have to shoot in the direction of the gun and assume they got Stagg," Captain Milton said.

"You think he's got a chance?" I asked.

"No, but that's why I'm a teacher," Milton answered. "Not a soldier."

We waited. Seconds passed, or maybe minutes, or maybe forever.

There were crickets in the area, and their calls brought a sense of normalcy to the night.

More time passed. Where the hell was Stagg? Gomez came up and said that the battalion was retreating.

"To where?" Milton asked.

"We pull back to this morning's line," Gomez said. "They called off the attack for tonight."

"What the hell does that mean?" Milton asked.

"It means, sir, that we, Baker Company of the 116th, are attacking the whole German army by ourselves," Gomez said. "Should we ask if they want to surrender?"

Captain Milton laughed. We all laughed. It was friggin' funny! What was left of our regiment, our battalion, our company, was a handful of men trying to stay alive, and we were all by ourselves leading the way against the German army. Sweet.

Gomez moved off to his position just as the big gun we had spotted fired a round. From where we were, we could smell the powder burning, could see the Krauts servicing the gun turn away from the muzzle blast, their white bodies orange and yellow reflecting the fire from the blast.

I could see the rear of the gun. It buckled and lurched after the shot, and I knew it had sent a shell toward our lines.

"We need to open up on the gun," I said.

"Wait a second," Captain Milton said.

"You sure?" I asked.

"Shut up!"

The gun fired again, and then there was a volley of small weapon fire, followed by silence.

We moved quickly along the edge of the tree line, angling upward on the terraced ridge, toward the German gun. It took a minute or so before we came across the bodies. One of the German soldiers was still alive. There were three already dead, two on one side of the big gun and one on the other. It was Milton who found Stagg. His body draped over a low branch, he looked as if he was searching for something on the ground, one arm extended forward and the other still clutching his M1.

Gomez collected the weapons of the Germans and we took cover. Milton said something about getting Stagg's body back, but we knew it was nonsense. The best we could manage was to drag him off the branch and cover him. I couldn't look at him, although I wanted to see his face one last time. Whatever his face looked like, it would be what mine would look like one day.

Petrocelli took something from the gun to make it inoperative, and we took positions in the dugouts the Germans had dug. The wounded Kraut signaled that he wanted some water, and Gomez gave him a drink from his canteen.

Milton was on the radio, giving our position, telling the CP that we were cut off.

"I think I'm overlooking St. Lo now," he said. "Yeah, I see a cathedral."

We spent the night on the ridge. Below us we could see the lights of vehicles gliding through the darkness. We were ten to fifteen feet apart, and Milton was trying to organize some sleeping time. He told me and Gomez to sleep first.

"How the hell we going to sleep?" Gomez asked. "You going to tuck us in?"

No answer from Milton.

The German started moaning, and Petrocelli asked him if he wanted us to kill him. I don't think he understood anything except Petrocelli's attitude, and I didn't think he cared anymore.

I don't know if I slept or not. I had kind of a dream, but it was an in-between fantasy, and I could have been awake. It was about me being surrounded by German soldiers who couldn't see me. I couldn't tell why they couldn't; they just seemed to ignore me. Then they stood up and started to leave, but before they did they came over to where I was and each shot me once. I didn't feel any pain, but I was terrified into wakefulness.

The wind picked up and it started raining again around the time I saw the first break in the distant sky.

"Something's coming!" Petrocelli whispered.

The sound of the engine whining as it switched gears climbing up the hill toward us was unnerving. They had probably tried to reach the gun crew by radio without luck and were now coming up to check on them.

The vehicle was small, about the size of a three-quarter-ton truck. There were two guys in the cab, and one got out the back. They seemed to disappear into the darkness.

"Gunther?" A low voice. "Baber?"

I thought of the wounded German soldier. Was he still alive? It had been a mistake not to kill him. Letting him live might be the death of us all.

A flashlight. It swept up the hill and stopped on the gun.

More conversation in German, and the Kraut soldiers started up toward the gun. They were still talking, not at all cautious.

When Petrocelli's grenade went off, I could see the first two German soldiers react. Their hands flew up and their bodies twisted from the impact. I opened fire at the last place I saw the third soldier, shooting almost blindly into the semigloom.

All three of the enemy were down. Milton went to them and disarmed them. I thought I heard a struggle. Was he killing them? I turned my attention away.

The first daylight and the Germans had been put in a pile in the shade of the gun. We had taken their water, and one of them had a hunk of cheese wrapped in cloth, which we split. There was some blood on the cloth and cheese, but Petrocelli cut it off with his bayonet before passing it out.

"We need to get away from the gun," Milton said. "They know where it is, or where it's supposed to be, and the next time they come looking for it they won't send careless people."

We looked for a sheltered way down the ridge and found one that looked promising. We hadn't gone more than fifty yards when we heard activity above us. Milton had been right. The Germans had sent a patrol out looking for the gun.

There was incoming artillery fire, and I imagined it was from our side. The Germans fooled around with the gun, I guessed trying to get it to fire, then moved down the ridge toward the town.

The rain started again. It was the seventeenth of July, and at noon, or at least close to it, a flight of light bombers came over and began bombing the town.

The bombing went on for thirty minutes and then left. Seconds later we heard the roar of heavy guns as our artillery began to pound St. Lo. You could actually see the shells flying overhead and into the town below. By three in the afternoon, the first American soldiers showed up from our rear. It was guys from First Army, and we were damned glad to see them.

I saw Mink talking to a sergeant and pointing toward the town. Captain Milton was talking to their officers, and I saw him go over to where we had left Stagg.

For a wild moment I thought I might have been wrong, that Stagg wasn't dead. When I saw them bring the wrapped body and put it on a truck, I knew it was for real.

The First Army guys set up a CP on the side of the hill away from the town, knowing that Kraut artillery would eventually answer our own. At 1600 hours, a food truck showed up.

I was so hungry and thirsty, my hands were shaking when I took the food from the cooks.

"You don't get this kind of chow in the 29th," a short, round-faced soldier said. "This is special First Army cuisine!"

By 1700 hours the Germans were shelling the hill with everything they had, and the First Army guys had moved back. Major Johns showed up from somewhere and told us to dig in.

"You guys did a great job! A great job! Charlie Company is going to attack in an hour from the west!" he said. The fool seemed almost cheerful about it.

Charlie Company, handfuls of half-starved soldiers the same as we were, didn't attack in an hour. The next two hours were an exchange of artillery and mortars. The rain had picked up, and it was too dark and wet for air coverage.

Captain Milton came over and told us that they had taken Stagg's body back for Graves Registration.

"I just wanted to let you guys know that," he said. "And we got another sergeant to take his place. They say he's having a little trouble."

"What kind of trouble?" Petrocelli asked.

"Just been in this war too long," Captain Milton said. "Just been in this war too long."

July 17 – Welcome to St. Lo

The new sergeant *was* weird. He was all, *"29, let's
go!" and talking about killing Nazis and strangling Hitler with his
bare hands. "If I could get my hands around that little bastard's neck,
I'd squeeze him until his eyeballs popped out!" Reese was a master
sergeant who had some years on him. I thought he had to be at least
pushing thirty-five, maybe forty even.

It was the first time I had heard anybody talking about Hitler
since we had left England. The English used to make fun of him in
the bars, calling him the Little Corporal. I never got the point of
that, but the Brits seemed to like it.

It was 2000 hours, and the Germans had figured out that we'd
taken the ridge overlooking St. Lo. They started shelling us with
everything they had: artillery, mortars, 88s. Guys were digging in

and holding on. For the first time, I didn't want to dig in. The ground began to shake all around me, but I didn't want to move.

"Woody, find some damned cover!" Captain Milton called to me as I sat on the ground, leaning against the wheel of a quarter ton.

He called to me again, and it was as if I couldn't hear him. I saw his mouth opening, and the agitation in his face, but I didn't hear anything he was saying. It was as if I was fogged over.

Then Mink was at my side with his arm around my shoulders. "Come on, Woody, we need to find some cover!" he said. "Let's find a ditch or something."

Yes. Suddenly I was clear again, and the sounds of the shells hitting the ground, the black smoke pouring up from the holes they had created, the shards of metal whistling past me and into the quarter ton, came back into focus.

Mink found an undercut ditch, and we huddled in it. I felt so tired, I just wanted to sleep.

"Don't sleep," Mink said. "In case they want to storm the ridge. They'll come in right after the barrage."

We waited. The shelling went on for another five minutes. The stink from the exploding shells was everywhere. Small patches of mist were forming at the top of the ridge, and I knew that if the Germans were coming, they would come through the same fog at the bottom of the ridge.

The artillery stopped. We grabbed our rifles and waited. Then it started again. They were playing with us. *Get ready to die, Americans.* The next shelling was different. The shells hit harder, and I imagined them to be from panzers. We didn't have anything to stop their tanks. Where the hell was our artillery? Why weren't we answering their attack?

The shelling stopped. We grabbed our rifles. I saw the medics on the move. More men had been wounded, more had died.

"Panzers!"

Reese was up and running toward the top of the ridge with a bazooka. If it was a self-propelled gun being driven up the mountain, he stood a chance. If it was a panzer, they would kill him instantly.

"You!" Reese pointed at me. "Grab these rockets!"

He had a bag of rockets for the bazooka. I got up and grabbed them. Six rockets, six shots. Nobody got off six shots against the Krauts. They were too good for that. You got off two if you were good, three if you were lucky.

I grabbed the bag of rockets and ran after Reese. We got to the top of the ridge, and he started aiming the bazooka.

Remembering what I had learned in basic, I took the first rocket out of the case, checked the tube of the bazooka to make sure it was clear, and then put in the shell. My hands were shaking so badly, I could hardly get the wires in to arm the damned thing. Finally the wires were in, and I tapped Sergeant Reese on the helmet.

I looked down the ridge and saw nothing but fog and smoke. Then I saw a belch of red-and-yellow flame and knew something had fired up the ridge.

The dark shadow that emerged could have been a self-propelled 88, or an antitank gun, or even a small tank. It wasn't one of their Tigers.

The blast from Reese's bazooka caught me by surprise. It shouldn't have. It burned the side of my face and my right ear.

"If it burns your left ear, it's because you're stupid and didn't think to get out of the back blast area!" the drill sergeant had said. *"If it burns your right ear, it's because you're stupid and didn't get out of the back blast area and you're a pussy hiding behind the shooter!"*

I loaded the bazooka again without looking down at the target. This time I was already clear when I tapped Sergeant Reese. His next shot hit the target, and I saw bodies flailing in the thick, heavy air. German soldiers were turning and offering their backs as targets.

The next rocket went in easier than the others, and Reese fired at something, I couldn't tell what, and then he stood up.

"That was for Major Howie," he said. There was anger boiling up in him, a kind of rage that only he knew about. "Did you know him?"

"No," I said.

"Fucking good man," Reese said. "Fucking good man."

We went back over the ridge where what was left of my battalion, my company, huddled and waited for more orders.

More artillery from our side. More mortars and then tracked antitank guns were being driven to the top of the ridge. The fog and smoke from the burning vehicles lifted, and I could see the wreckage we had caused. There were dead and wounded soldiers strewn between the half-burned trees. We had beaten off a suicide attack. They had to know they were going to die, running up the hill while we were shooting down at them. They had to know.

In the distance we could see mortars coming in from the far side of the town. There were fires everywhere and dark angry clouds of black smoke lifting angrily into the morning sky.

The food truck had got through, but without its food. It had been hit by a shell, and all the food had been scattered on the road. They had managed to save some chicken soup.

It was the best chicken soup that God had ever sent to earth.

At 1200 hours, our artillery began to bombard St. Lo. We could see the shells hitting, and Captain Milton was running around, telling us to get ready to attack.

"We going down there?" Sergeant Reese asked.

"We haven't been given orders to move," Milton said. "But the shelling has to be for something!"

"Where you from?" Gomez asked Sergeant Reese.

"Racine, Wisconsin."

"What's going on in Racine?"

"Americans," Reese answered. "Americans are going on."

■　■　■

The shelling went on forever. Not for a while, but forever. From the ridge we could occasionally see a Kraut running from one building to another.

"They look like roaches!" Reese said.

To me they looked like men running for their lives, with no place to run to.

"You people know what happened?" Reese asked. "You know that Major Howie was killed? Did you know that?"

We had heard, but nobody spoke up. Major Howie had meant something to Reese, and we didn't want to take that away. I was hoping that if I got it, if I was lying somewhere faceup to the foggy Normandy sky, that someone would be upset. I wondered who it would be.

Shut up, mind. Stop thinking about it.

"Typhoons!" This from Petrocelli. "Thank God they're on our side."

I looked up and saw the British fighter planes coming in formation, then peeling off for bombing runs. A Kraut gunner sent a stream of cannon fire into the sky. I could see the tracer bullets going straight up and then arcing downward. The Brit fliers came down with a vengeance, blasting anything moving, bombing anything they thought might have been a likely target. The rockets from the Typhoons tore into the buildings, sending ugly sprays of black-and-yellow flames high into the air over the carcasses and bodies already lying there.

We were being rallied again. Captain Milton was pointing down the ridge into the city. I knew the Krauts, by instinct, by command, would send shells our way as we went toward the town.

Mink and I started down together. Ahead of us, a .30 caliber machine gun over his right shoulder, was Reese.

"I think he's losing it!" I said to Mink.

"I hope he doesn't find it!" Mink answered.

What the hell did that mean?

■ ■ ■

In ten minutes we were in St. Lo. This is what we had been fighting for the past month. Gerhardt had been pushing us, telling us how disappointed he was in us because we hadn't taken St. Lo. And now we had taken it.

But there was no St. Lo.

There were the remnants of a city: torn-up buildings, a post office's white walls pockmarked by a hundred — no, a thousand — shells. Fragments of walls and horizontal lines that were life markers and stories in people's lives. There were animals lying dead in the streets. Some, which had been there for days, already bloated and stinking. There were burned-out German vehicles, some with the bodies of their drivers still in them, alongside the buildings. They, too, looked like dead animals.

We moved into the center of the city cautiously, in two groups, past an old railroad station, a shop front that Mink identified as once having been a bakery, and piles and piles of rubble. Some of the men were sent from house to house, looking for Krauts who hadn't been killed and who hadn't fled. Some were found. A few were captured. Most were killed. It was a matter of who had won and who had lost. Now *we* were the children with murderous eyes.

"Let's go into the cathedral," Mink said to me.

"Why?"

"I don't know," he said. "Maybe we can build memories better than the ones we stumble on."

I didn't want to go into the cathedral, and I shouldn't have. Inside it was nothing but rubble, twisted wood where pews had been, an altar completely burned through one side but neat and gilded on the other. We picked our way around, and Mink pointed out a plaster fresco of cherubs and a figure on one of them.

"'And he rode upon the cherubs, and flew upon the wind.'"

"Mink, don't go deep on me," I said. "I'm too tired."

"So let's go find some sleep," he answered.

We got back to where Johns was re-forming the battalion again. He was asking each officer to give him a count of the men, and he was shocked to see how few of us were left. He told us to find an area of the city that seemed safe from incoming artillery and set out guards.

We collapsed in houses along the street that led to the ruined train depot. Some guys fell asleep, but I couldn't. It was almost as if I had forgotten how. I tried to figure out if I was hungry, couldn't, and just assumed I must be. Then we were up again. A bugle blew that told us it was time for something. A bugle? We were forming companies and squads, and I wondered what the hell was going on.

Major Johns had us forming a square that was more or less in the middle of the town away from the depot. There was a flag-draped body on a mound of rubble.

"That's Major Howie," Burns said.

"Who the hell was he?" Gomez asked.

"A believer, I guess." Burns looked away. "A believer."

We were lined up in a square, and I thought about the people I knew who had been believers. Stagg, Duncan, Freihofer, Arness . . .

"Men of the 29th Infantry Regiment, today we have achieved our goal, the taking of this city, the taking of St. Lo, which the enemy has defended so well and with such determination. They thought that they would defeat us by making the price too high, by making the task too difficult, by making us doubt our purpose. But they have not defeated us. We have prevailed. Let no man or no citizen ever forget that fact. We have prevailed!"

General Gerhardt stood in front of the body of men, the survivors from Bedford and from Maryland, and spit out his words as if he were talking to children back in Virginia.

"Let no one forget that we stormed the beaches at Normandy armed primarily with our courage and the certain knowledge that we would defeat the Nazi war machine! Let no one forget what we have accomplished here today and what we will accomplish in the future. I leave you with this message, and with this message only: *29, let's go!*"

There was the Presentation of Colors, and we raised the American flag on the clock of the church in the square. A few Frenchwomen were brought into the square and presented us with a bottle of wine and a few loaves of French bread. Then General Gerhardt's jeep was brought up, with D-Day in the backseat, and he was whisked off.

We relaxed, but I could feel the tension in the air. We had taken St. Lo, but there was no town here. Notre-Dame Cathedral, where Major Howie's body was put on display, was a shell, a place where no God would live. We hadn't liberated anything, or anyone. We had destroyed the city, killed or chased away most of the people in it, and were claiming a victory.

"Mink, is this what war is about?" I asked. "Why the hell are we doing this?"

" 'Theirs not to reason why,' " Mink answered. " 'Theirs but to do and die.' "

"What the hell does that mean?"

"It's the substance of war," Mink said. "Can't you taste it?"

"You're cracking up," I said.

Captain Milton found us and told us that we were going to be moving out of St. Lo at sundown.

"In case there's a German counterattack," he said. "Gerhardt wants the troops dispersed around the town. Their artillery, what's left of it, has probably got the main parts of the town zeroed in, so we'll move to the outskirts."

"Why don't we just give it back to them?" Petrocelli asked. "It would serve the bastards right to have to move back into this piece of crap!"

Captain Milton looked at Petrocelli and shrugged.

"Food coming in!" a corporal from the First Army called.

There were four deuce and a halfs pulling up in the town square in front of a building called *Boulangerie*. I was right there with Gomez and Mink, wanting some warm food for a change, and I watched as the trucks pulled up and the drivers got out.

Guys started forming a line even before the food was set up, and we had to watch while the food service guys set up stoves and GI cans of hot steamy water and brought out cases of rations.

"I don't know if I want to eat most or take a bath most," Petrocelli said.

"If you don't eat first, I'll eat your food," Gomez said, which settled the matter.

The food was glorious. It was mashed potatoes, peas, and some real some-kind-of-meat in gravy that spilled over onto the potatoes and peas in a way that only the angels could have arranged. We got as much as we wanted, and some guys were close to crying it was so good, and we were so hungry.

The ice cream came in little packs, and we were each given two packs and something that tasted like fruit.

"This is peaches, Mink," I said. "No, really, it is real peaches!"

"You ever think a peach could taste so good?" he asked.

"And I didn't think . . . No, I guess not," I said.

I thought about going back for more. I wasn't hungry any longer — the first few bites had me filled — but I wanted to keep the moment going, to make it last.

"Gomez is screwed up!" Petrocelli said, walking up to us. He had his helmet hanging off his head.

"He bought it?"

"No, but it's almost as bad." Petrocelli looked worried. "Come on and talk to him with me."

Petrocelli didn't look good, either. He led the way, with me on his heels and Mink behind us, over to where some men stood around the back of a truck. On the ground, looking smaller than I had ever seen him, was Gomez. The tears were streaming down his cheeks and his face was distorted, as if he was feeling some pain somewhere but it just wasn't clear where.

Kneeling by his side, I put my hand on his shoulder.

"What's going on, buddy?"

"The fucking Krauts shot up the mail truck!" Gomez said. "They wasted the damned mail truck! Why the hell did they have to do that? *Why?*"

I could feel for Gomez. We were cut off from everything that was important to us. There was an ocean between us and the world that made sense.

There was nothing I could say to Gomez that made things better. We had fought for that damned mail. And now the Krauts had blown it up or burned it up or captured it or —

I asked Gomez if they had destroyed the mail or captured it.

"The black guys ran into an 88 sitting on the roadside. Killed everyone on two friggin' trucks," he said. "The mail and medical supplies burned up."

Crap.

I imagined the letter from Vernelle. What would she say? That she loved me and was thinking so hard about me that it gave her headaches? Maybe she had been thinking of making me a peach pie when I got home. What would she say?

I wanted to hear her voice in my head so bad, it made my stomach turn knowing that it wouldn't happen. The words would be enough to get the sound of her voice — I didn't remember it, but in my mind it was sweet and soft, like the early morning breezes lifting off the fields around Bedford. Like the smell of fresh baked goods and preserves in the back of the car as we drove up from the Roanoke State Fair.

It was okay, though. As long as Vernelle didn't mind waiting for me to be finished with this war, it would be okay. There wouldn't be a lot I could offer her at first, I knew, but I would bring something back from Normandy, and from all of this fighting, and from all of this wondering who I was. I'd find something to bring back.

July 20, or Maybe the 21st, 1944

We lost another medic in the afternoon. He had been wounded earlier and tried to ignore it, but it caught up with him. Losing a medic was hard because you depended on them. Not when you were hit or down, but when you were running across a field knowing that any moment you could be lying on your back trying to suck air through a bloody wound or looking into the faces of the men around you to see if they thought you were going to make it. You needed someone you could rely on, or at least think would save your life if you got hit.

"Make sure your canteens are filled with water, and that you're carrying all the food you can," Captain Milton said. "We don't want to get caught out there without food and water again!"

"Yo, Captain, when does the last bus leave for Coney Island?" Burns asked.

"You ever been to Coney Island?" Captain Milton asked. "I was there once with my wife. It's a wild place. We must have dropped twenty-five dollars in half a day!"

"You got kids?" I asked.

"No, have you?" Captain Milton asked me. "You got any kids?"

"No, but I think I got a wife lined up," I said. "It's a could-be kind of thing."

"Wish you luck with it, soldier."

It was 1800 hours, and we were getting ready to move out once it got dark. I didn't like that. The Krauts were scared to be on the road during the daylight hours and everybody knew it. They could fight from the hedgerows all they wanted, but our Mustangs and the Canadian Typhoons would pound anything we targeted and the entire German army knew that. Their Luftwaffe was mostly gone.

1900 hours. We were sitting around, and I was asking myself if I needed to go to the bathroom. There were a couple of toilets in St. Lo that weren't blown up, but there were lines for them. Most of the guys were just finding corners to crap in if they had to go. A major came by and handed out captured German weapons.

"This is a *panzerschreck*! It's like our bazooka," he said. "Wouldn't you just love to knock out one of their tanks with their own weapon?"

No. Nobody said anything, but we were all thinking *no*, and the major moved on pretty quick. I had filled my canteen with water, as Captain Milton had recommended, and also filled a canteen I had found. The second one I put in my backpack. I wanted to take some extra food with me, but I knew none of it would last. Burns had once said that in a pinch we could butcher some of the dying animals. That didn't go over too well, not even among the farm boys.

My mind drifted back to Vernelle, what she was thinking, and what she was thinking about me.

"Hey, Mink, I told you a little about Vernelle back home," I said. "You think she'll wait for me?"

"She have a choice?" Mink asked.

"Not really, physically," I said. "But do you think she'll want to have something more going on with me?"

"Could be," Mink said. "I was thinking of writing to a girl back home."

"You got a girl?"

"No, but that doesn't stop me from dreaming," Mink answered.

"I guess we're all dreaming," I said. "Even getting home —"

"*Gott helfen Sie mir! Gott helfen Sie mir!*"

From the restaurant, from the very restaurant that we had lined up in front of to hear General Gerhardt's speech, came three Germans. Two of them were in uniforms, one with a bayonet on which he had tied a white undershirt. He was giving up.

The third one was stark naked. The first two were trying to cover the third guy with an overcoat.

"*Gott helfen Sie mir! Gott helfen Sie mir!*"

Some of the guys were stunned; others jumped up and trained their guns on the Kraut soldiers. The guys from the 29th made motions for the Krauts to lift their arms higher, and they did, dropping the bayonet and undershirt.

The other man fell to his knees, lifting his arms to the skies, and calling out again.

"Gott helfen Sie mir! Gott helfen Sie mir!"

"Who speaks German? Who speaks German?" Master Sergeant Reese looked around. Nobody answered.

He spoke to the German soldiers. "You speak English?"

"We surrender! We surrender!"

"What's his story?" Reese had the muzzle of his M1 under the naked German's nose.

"Too much for his head," the German said. "Too much for his head."

"Gott helfen Sie mir! Gott helfen Sie mir!"

"What is he saying?"

"I think he's asking God to help him," Mink said. "He's looking for his lost saints. Maybe it's too late for even God to help him now."

It was shocking to know that there were still Germans so close to us. But the naked Kraut was even more of a surprise. We looked at him tearing at his hair and tossing his head back and forth. He was completely naked, his body white and filthy, his ribs prominent as if he maybe hadn't eaten for a while. But his eyes were the worst. He was looking around him wildly, and then back over his shoulder, his mouth agape as if there were visions only he could see.

"Sag das nicht! Sag das nicht!"

"What's he saying?"

"He is hearing voices." The Kraut soldier with the crazed man shrugged and tapped his head.

Our guys started looking away.

" 'It crack'd and growl'd, and roar'd and howled, Like noises in a swound!' " This from Mink.

"You say anything else and I'll shoot you myself," I hissed at Mink. I didn't want any more of his damned poems or his insights or his wisdom. It was wrong, but I didn't want any more thinking.

Some of our guys helped carry the Kraut soldier off. He looked at them as if they, too, were some kind of weird beast that he hadn't seen before. But somehow we knew what he was, and what he was going through.

We had to do a sweep of the buildings in the area, and two more Germans, one badly wounded and nearly dead, were found.

"Good thing these guys didn't waste us when we were prancing around in formation," Burns said. "We're just fucking lucky! Fucking lucky!"

We began to assemble our gear to move out. The day was drawing to a close, and the sky behind St. Lo was an eerie silver, not gray or blue, but the color of an old urn. The buildings, or what was left of them, seemed like so many quick charcoal drawings that would be finished in a mythical time and place.

Pushing. I felt myself pushing the image of the Kraut soldier out of my mind. I didn't want that to be me, to be me looking for my lost saints or my lost salvation.

Pushing. No, not pushing, but trying not to think.

"Hey, Mink, you ever try not to think?" I asked.

"If you fill your head with poems, you don't have to think," Mink said. "The rhymes and the rhythms and the music of it all can fill the soul."

"You believe that?"

"No, man." Mink's smile broadened. "But ain't it a grand thing to be saying?"

Guys were scrounging extra ammunition and extra food to carry out into the field. I found a case with four little jars of slide grease and put them into my pocket. I didn't know why, but it seemed like a good idea at the time.

"Coloreds," Captain Milton said. "It's always good to see them because they're bringing something we can use."

Looking up, I saw some black soldiers securing their trucks. Then I saw someone I thought I recognized. I looked closer and a warm feeling came over me. I got to my feet and went over to the last truck from the end.

"Yo, Marcus!"

Marcus Perry turned toward me and then looked past me. I watched as he secured the back tarp of his deuce and a half.

"How are things going, man?" I asked.

"What you want?" he grunted more than spoke.

"To say hello," I said. "How you doing?"

"Yeah, hello." Another grunt.

I had read in *Stars and Stripes* how a lot of the black soldiers were getting pissed because of segregation. I hadn't thought much about it, but I knew it was going on. The Army was the Army, I thought. Maybe life wasn't perfect, but it was never perfect. I didn't think Marcus would turn away from me.

What difference did it make? I went back to where Mink and Gomez were packing up their gear and started to try to think about where we were going next. I didn't want to think about what was going through Mink's head, and I didn't want to think about what was going through Marcus's. *The hell with both of them,* I thought.

Captain Milton had shown us a map that hadn't made a lot of sense to me. The map laid out yards and miles. The drawings showed fields as if they were gardens. The distances between cities, cities close enough to see from town square to town square, were real on the maps but unreal in what I was calling life.

"Hey, excuse me!"

I turned and saw Marcus looking at me. "What?"

"Where you from?"

"Forget about it," I said.

"No, no . . . you from Bedford?" Marcus asked. "In Virginia?"

"Yeah."

"Josiah?" He looked closely at me. "You're Josiah, right?"

He hadn't recognized me! Marcus hadn't fucking recognized me!

"Yeah, I'm Josiah," I said. "Josiah Wedgewood!"

"Oh, man. Oh, man." Marcus put his arms around me and pulled me to his chest.

"Okay! Okay! Let's move it out! Four hundred seventy-seven miles we got to fucking go before we fucking sleep! Let's go!"

"How are things going at home?" I asked Marcus.

"Not good, Mama says," Marcus answered. "They're grieving about what's happened to us over here."

"They know we're winning?" I asked.

"They're too simple to know that," Marcus said. "To the folks back home, dying is losing."

Marcus kissed me on the forehead. It was the first time I remember being kissed by a grown man. It felt good, and, as we held hands, there was meaning to it. There was Bedford, and family, and friendship, and all kinds of kin stuff. I was sorry about him being black, or maybe about the way we had treated blacks. Maybe after the war it would be different.

"Take care of yourself, man," he said. "Take good care."

"You do the same, Marcus," I said.

The trucks started moving out, and I waved good-bye to Marcus. I thought I saw his hand go up, and I kept waving until I couldn't see the cab of his deuce and a half any longer.

The Colored supply trucks moved out, and then some more trucks came in and a handful of Shermans.

"Mount up, 29th! We've moving out!"

The word was already out that we were moving toward Sainte-Marguerite-d'Elle. I was sitting on the back of a Sherman with Mink.

"Two days, Woody," Mink said. "Major Johns's orderly said we'd be there for two days for R & R, and then we'd be on reserve for the 30th. How can they take us out for only two damned days?"

"Mink, Marcus didn't recognize me," I said. "We grew up in the same town and went down the same streets. We know the same people. How could he not recognize me?"

"Maybe he was tired," Mink said. "How long is it to Marguerite-d'Elle?"

"It took a week to fight our way here," I said. "We must have killed half the Germans in the world to get to St. Lo."

"At least."

"How could he not recognize me?" I wanted to get a mirror and look at myself. I wanted to see what my face was like and my eyes. I ran my hands over my face to see what it felt like.

"Mink, how many Germans do you think there are?"

A whistle. Incoming artillery. The Shermans started off the road, and we were at an angle, being brushed off by the branches along the hedgerow.

I was on the ground when the first shells hit too far to the right. We found what shelter we could and held our breath.

"This is all supposed to be clear," Captain Milton was shouting. "But be on alert in case there are some die-hard assholes who need killing!"

We waited for five minutes, and all the artillery was wide. Then the shelling stopped and we could see shells going in the opposite direction. Our guys were answering back.

"They're still spotting from the ridges around St. Lo," Gomez said. "There's still a few of them left around there."

We were less than two miles from Sainte-Marguerite-d'Elle, and the whole thing seemed stupid. Where was the safe area? Where were we going to go where there was no fighting?

We were sitting around waiting for orders again. Move up. Move back. Get bored and then run for your life. It was a crazy way to live.

I thought of Vernelle and wondered if she would ever be waiting for me in a man-woman kind of way. Maybe Marcus would get back first and he would tell her that I looked different.

"He's a little meaner-looking," Marcus would say. And Vernelle would understand. She'd nod a little nod that I'd given her in my mind, her dark hair setting off her eyes just right and a slightly worried look on her face. Maybe there would even be a tear in her eye, or at least the little lines between her eyes would furrow and maybe her hands would tense up.

A thought came that maybe none of this would happen, but I quickly pushed it out of my mind. I wanted it to happen. It would happen if I needed it to.

On the road again. This time we packed up and got in a tank convoy. The tanks were moving slower, and we were all on trucks or on half-tracks traveling between them. Riding was so much better than walking, and I was bouncing along next to Mink.

"Hey, Mink, you got any happy poems in your head?" I asked. "Something that's going to make me feel good?"

"I think it's the sadness of poems that touches the heart," Mink said. "But I have one that makes me feel good."

"Spit it out!"

"'No Man Is an Island,'" Mink said, then cleared his throat before going on. "'No man is an island, Entire of itself. Each is a piece of the continent, A part of the main. If a clod be washed away by the sea, Europe is the less —'"

"Planes!"

"They got to be ours!"

"Krauts!"

The first shells hit the guys ahead of us, and we started dashing for cover. I turned back and looked over my shoulder. They were Krauts. Three pitiful Kraut planes silhouetted against the darkening sky, the flak exploding around them.

One of them suddenly burst into flames, and another veered off sharply to avoid the debris.

We were in a clearing fifty yards from the woods, and we ran toward them. There was a ditch in front of a hedgerow, and I could feel my legs strain as I made for it.

Suddenly I felt something go wrong in my back, and my right leg began to go crazy. I could still run, but stupidly, and I hit the ditch and fell heavily onto my chest. I thought I might have been hit. I saw Mink just in front of me.

"Mink! Mink! Check out my leg. I think I'm hit!"

The leg was jerking badly, and I knew I wasn't jerking it. It felt like it was broken.

I was on my back and I saw another of the Kraut planes go up in smoke and another peel off and fly away into the night sky.

"Mink, take a look at my leg," I said, reaching for him. "I don't want to look."

Mink's head was down, and I pulled at his shoulder.

Mink's head was down, and I pulled.

Mink's head was down.

I turned him around, but I already knew. There was a huge hole in his chest.

"Oh, Mink. Oh, Mink . . ."

Epilogue – November 23, 1944

There are a few snow flurries mixed in with the rain, and the wide grounds outside of the medical center in Blandford Forum, England, are empty. The grass and trees are still a bright, bright green, and through the mist they seem almost to shimmer in the morning air. I had hoped to have been back in the States by now, but my leg, which had been healing, has an infection. A bullet nicked my femur and shattered it. At first they thought that I would be able to return to my unit, but when the healing took too long they said I'd probably be reassigned to a Headquarters Company. The doctor, a bright little man, said that the only real danger was that the healing would be uneven and my right leg would become shorter than my left.

"If that happens, your ballet days will be over," he jokes.

It's Thanksgiving Day, and we are told there will be services for the American soldiers. Catholics at seven and ten and Protestants in the afternoon. It's not a holiday for the Brits, and some of them kid us about what they call the War of Rebellion.

They have brought American newspapers as well as the usual British papers and pass them out in the dining hall. I've a wheelchair and sit with some paratroopers to eat my eggs, toast, and fat English sausages, which I don't like.

I look through the papers, reading the *Mirror* first, and then the *Sun*. I save the *New York Times* for my bed. What I want to see are the sports news and the local New York happenings. It's funny how cheering those kinds of things can be. I glance at the paper in the dining room and am shocked to see a mention of the 29th on the front page.

I get myself back to my bed, easing my leg up onto the bed and into the sling they've rigged for me. The paper is the Late City Edition, and there is a picture of Eisenhower talking to a group of soldiers. The caption reads: GENERAL DWIGHT D. EISENHOWER TALK-ING TO MEMBERS OF THE 29TH INFANTRY DIVISION DURING HIS VISIT TO THE FRONT LINES.

They were in Germany!

I am so pleased for them. I feel like laughing and crying at the same time. These are my guys, the ones I had fought with and suf-fered with, and finally they were being given some real recognition. I want to save the paper forever.

Ten thirty and a group of soldiers, clean-cut and shaven, come in. They have cameras, and I know they're from either *Stars and Stripes* or some other paper doing a story about how well we are being treated for the folks back home. There is a young civilian woman with them, a real looker and she knows it, and she comes to my bed and asks my name, outfit, and hometown.

"Josiah Wedgewood, from Bedford, Virginia," I say, "29th Infantry."

"Oh!" She looks surprised. "How are you doing?"

"I'm doing good," I answer. "I see some of our guys made the front page of the *New York Times*."

She takes the paper and looks at it approvingly.

"How would you sum up the accomplishments of the 29th Infantry?" she asks.

I search for an answer, and then I get all emotional and have to blink away the tears. A fool with a camera snaps my picture, but the girl motions for him to put the camera down.

"Can we come back a little later?" she asks. She has a sweet voice.

"Yeah, sure," I say.

She pats my good leg and leads the others out of the ward.

"You need to get up a list of good things to say, mate," says a Canadian soldier who lost part of his right arm. "Then whenever they ask, you can just pick one of them."

"Yeah."

The Canadian starts to shave, and I realize he's still working on teaching himself to shave with the hand he has left. I start thinking about what I will say if the girl does come back.

Mink would have known what to say to her. He would have closed his eyes for a moment and then pulled something from his mind that was half poetry and right on the money. He would have looked at the picture of Ike on the front cover of the *Times* and seen more than me and captured it in a few words. Mink brought words to the war. Some of them I hadn't wanted to hear because the truth wasn't something I always wanted to deal with.

The words don't come easy for me. When I wrote to my mom, I found myself worrying about things not to tell her. The thing is that I can't say things about the dying and make it sound like anything except the horrible idea it is. When you see a soldier — someone who was alive a few hours or a few minutes or a few seconds ago — crushed in the track of a tank, or charred and smoldering on the side of the road, it's a shock that you just don't fit in easily. You need special words to say those things, and you know other people won't understand them, because you don't bring a lot of understanding to them yourself.

Vernelle would be easier, I thought. But there were three letters I started to write to her to tell her what had happened to my leg and what had happened to my friend Mink. The letters were awkward; the sentences didn't fit what I was feeling at the time.

I want to say good things when I describe the men I fought alongside. When Stagg ran up the hill after the Kraut gun, when he took out the German crew and gave up his own life, he was bigger than I can ever be, and he needs to be talked about. Somebody needs to write down that he reached inside of himself in that moment and found something greater and larger than even the possibility of his own survival. And when Duncan and Arness and so many others had bought it on Omaha Beach, had died struggling just to get to the shore so that they could fight — somebody needs to put it into words. For most of us that day it was just a matter of trying to hold down the fear, of trying not to call out for our mothers, maybe even trying not to face the naming of what was going on.

There should be something special to say about having the guts to get up and run across a field toward another hedgerow. And there should be something to say about killing people you didn't know.

When you were there, when you held your M1 in your hand with your heart beating a mile a damned minute and you were facing someone who wanted to kill you, it was one experience. But later, when you were away from them and thinking back without the panic in your throat and the sweat dripping down your face, the same experience was different. Different because it came with the realization that you *could* kill. There is no training in killing. They didn't hold up anyone like Rudolf, the prisoner Helmut's brother, for us to shoot in basic. There were just round targets to shoot at on sunny days in Virginia and Maryland and Georgia as we got ready.

June sixth changed us all. It made us into something else, something that could kill in the constant anxiety of battle. We were able to reach deep into ourselves and find the beasts within and bring them out so that we could survive. How could we put words to that feeling, or that beast? How could we tell anybody about how hard it was to put the beast back inside our hearts, and bodies, and souls, once we knew it lived there?

Maybe Mink could have collected the words and put them down, but even with Mink I wasn't sure. For me, my memories are already changing what I saw and what I've done. The visions are already getting softer, less hard-edged. Scenes I thought I would never forget are beginning to fade and fold into other scenes, are becoming less violent, and I know that I don't want to sort them out, I don't want to relive them, and, yes, I don't want to find the right words to make them real again. What I need is for the running across the beach, the calling out for God, the fear, the pain, and, most of all, the killing to become somehow bearable. Somehow bearable.

If any of the dead returned — Major Howie, Stagg, the bodies bobbing in the water — perhaps they could be clearer, or would want to be. Or perhaps if the German soldier, naked and beyond his senses, could have translated for us the voices he heard when he was calling out "Don't say that!" over and over again, maybe if we could have all heard what he didn't want us to say, it would have been meaningful.

After I was wounded, some of the guys found the impromptu aid station where they had taken me and I had promised them I would write. I haven't. I've promised myself I would write to Marcus or, barring that, would sit down with him when I got home — if he also made it back — and have a beer. Now, I'm not sure.

If I connect with Vernelle, I'll give her a version of what I have been through. Mom will get another version, and then I'll probably just keep my mouth shut and the beasts I have seen shut away.

The girl comes back and announces that she's from a news service.

"We reach over sixty papers in the States," she says. "Could you tell me, and all America, what you are feeling now that you have seen General Eisenhower commend the troops you fought with?"

"I'm proud of the 29th, and of all the men I served with," I say. "They're a great bunch of guys."

"I thank you, sir," she says. "I thank you, and the country thanks you."

She pats the leg in the sling and leaves.

Author's Note
THE BONES OF WAR

It wasn't easy talking to the veterans of World War II, or reading their letters, or probing their feelings. I talked to most of them multiple times, and they gave me as much information as they could remember, often becoming quite emotional as they talked about the June 1944 invasion of Europe. Some of them wept as they spoke. I thought I knew how they felt.

My first book about war dealt with the death of my brother in Vietnam. His death was the kind of shock that no one is ever fully prepared for. I started writing a short story about what I was doing the moment that Sonny was killed. It helped some, but then I wrote another story, which I published in *Essence* magazine. Finally, I approached the Vietnam story in the form of a novel, *Fallen Angels*. It was the hardest book I had ever written. I didn't think that I would ever write another book about war.

Then my oldest son, a military chaplain, called to say that he was going with his unit to the Middle East. The research for *Sunrise over Fallujah* was a kind of preparation for the bad news, which, fortunately, never came. Michael Dean Myers survived, but both he and I were changed by what was known as the Gulf War; he by what he saw and experienced, and I by the realization that no amount of clever talk, no amount of high-level policy meetings, would ever do away with man's capacity for self-destruction.

I took Robin Perry — the nephew of Richard Perry, a character in *Fallen Angels* — and put him in the center of *Sunrise*. Yes, Vietnam was different than Iraq, the weapons and terrain were dissimilar, but I needed to show that they shared the same brutal ideas, the same need for young people to come to grips with who they are and to face the fundamental need for survival while doing their duty. In *Sunrise* the relationship between Robin Perry as he serves in Iraq and his father and uncle back home has a kind of tension that comes with the fear of having a loved one in combat. As long as my son was in the combat area I feared for his safety. Every phone call in the middle of the night filled me with alarm. This is the nature of war.

World War II ended with the unconditional surrender of the Germans and the devastating bombing of Japan. I remember thinking that there would probably be no more wars after the nuclear blasts in Hiroshima and Nagasaki. But wars are started by people, not weapons. In *Invasion* I created a character, Marcus Perry, who was the father and uncle to those who served in subsequent wars. He is serving in a segregated army and does not fight with Josiah "Woody" Wedgewood, a young man from his hometown of Bedford, Virginia. The two friends carry the traditions of their own country into a worldwide conflict as both risk their lives fighting against the Nazis.

The basic truth about war is that it is unbelievably brutal and I want my readers to understand this. When we sift through the images to find one suitable to publish, as we put background scenes and sounds to men running across open fields, we tend to put away those pictures we don't want to see. If we're lucky we can put a face on war that reveals its horrors, but in a way that doesn't repulse the reader. It's not an easy task because we know too much about what happens on the battlefields.

We know that the bombs we drop on cities will kill civilians as well as soldiers. We know that children, even babies, will die. We know that some of our friends will not return. We know that many who do return will be strangers to us.

When General Dwight D. Eisenhower sent American soldiers off to storm Omaha Beach he knew that many of the over fifty thousand American troops, perhaps up to 70 percent of the first wave, would be either killed or wounded. How can we even think of that many young lives lost? And yet Eisenhower had to make that decision.

"We saw our boys dying on the beach," ex–Navy officer Henry B. McFarland told me. "And we knew we had to get our ships in as close to the beach as possible — the bottoms were scraping sand — to fire back at the German guns."

The Germans were expecting the attack, and their general Erwin Rommel knew how important the beach landings would be. Everyone knew about the dying that would happen that day. By June 1944 it was clear that Germany was losing the war, but there were madmen who insisted the carnage continue. Hitler called upon old men and young boys to sacrifice their lives for his lost cause.

"I was fifteen," a former German soldier told me. "I was scared to go into the war, but I was just as scared to say that I wouldn't."

I asked John Cingerre, who had been among the first waves onto Omaha, how tired he had been at the end of what has become known as the Longest Day. "I was exhausted, but I couldn't sleep," he said. "I was just looking all around me, at all the dead bodies and all the wounded men, and wondered if I would make it out alive."

I asked William H. Edwards about his experiences as a truck driver, bringing supplies to the front lines under heavy fire. "The Germans knew that the ammunition and equipment we were bringing from the beach to the front was crucial, and they sent out sniper teams to kill the drivers," he said. "I was driving in a convoy at night, inches from the truck in front of me, and trying to steer from the center seat. It was some scary times."

The men stood up under the pressure of having to fight across the hedgerows of Normandy. They quickly understood what the costs would be in human suffering and losses and were willing to make the sacrifices. But there was a sense of loss that stayed with them forever. Corporal Albert C. Wehmeyer wrote to a young woman that his brother had met briefly, and had shared his brother's feelings about their possible future together. The brother had been killed in Normandy.

"I am trying to find out where he is buried, but as yet I haven't been able to but hope to soon. . . . I was very lucky to get to see him about three weeks before it happened. I shall never forget those last twenty minutes we spent together."

Ironically, it was the young people of the Second World War era who made the decisions to fight in Vietnam. And it was the young people of the Vietnam War era who made many of the decisions to fight in the Middle East. Will there ever be an end to war? Perhaps. Perhaps if we don't make the killing attractive, if we give accurate pictures of the horrors involved, if we can get our young men and women to look for other ways of settling disputes, it might end.

Acknowledgments
TRUE COLORS

I received brilliant support in my reserach for this book, among which were interviews granted by Henry B. McFarland, who, on June 6, 1944, was a young Naval officer supporting the initial assault on Omaha Beach. He also supplied me with the invasion maps. John Cingerre was an enlisted man struggling to get a foothold on the beach and described, in detail, the dreadful scenes of bravery and horror, as well as the difficult days that followed. The only frontline African American soldiers landing on June 6 were those involved in setting up the barrage balloons that protected the ground troops from enemy aircraft. William H. Edwards, in a largely African American Transportation Battalion, arrived on June 7 and, with great emotion, told me of his part in the war as a member of the famed Red Ball Express — the truck convoys that supplied the American Army as it tried to break a determined German Resistance.

The photograph that is used in the background of this book's cover is one I supplied from my personal collection. For inclusion on the cover, its background has been slightly cropped. The photo was taken on June 7, 1944. In the original photo, there are long lines of men who have been off-loaded onto Omaha Beach, and the offshore Naval vessels have moved in closer to shore. On June 7, transportation units, stevedores, Graves Registration, and other support units were all coming ashore. This is why I chose to put Perry in a transportation unit. The African American soldier

I interviewed, William H. Edwards, landed (along with his assistant driver) on this day.

The Army was officially integrated in 1948, but black soldiers were brought from the Pacific campaign on a volunteer basis and put into white units in 1945. This was done without fanfare because of the need for warm bodies.